The
SWEET
LIFE
of
Stella
Madison

The SWEET LIFE of Stella Madison

· · ·

LARA M. ZEISES

DELACORTE PRESS

Copyright © 2009 by Lara M. Zeises

All rights reserved. Published in the United States by Delacorte Press, an imprint of Random House Children's Books, a division of Random House, Inc., New York. Originally published in hardcover in the United States by Delacorte Press in 2009.

Delacorte Press is a registered trademark and the colophon is a trademark of Random House, Inc.

Visit us on the Web! www.randomhouse.com/teens
Educators and librarians, for a variety of teaching tools,
visit us at www.randomhouse.com/teachers

The Library of Congress has cataloged the hardcover edition of this work as follows:
The Sweet Life of Stella Madison / Lara Zeises.   p.   cm.
Summary: Seventeen-year-old Stella struggles with the separation of her renowned chef parents, writing a food column for the local paper even though she is a junk food addict, and having a boyfriend but being attracted to another.
ISBN 978-0-385-73146-1 (hc)—ISBN 978-0-385-90178-9 (glb)
ISBN 978-0-375-89266-0 (e-book)
[1. Family problems—Fiction.   2. Food—Fiction.
3. Dating (Social customs)—Fiction.   4. Interpersonal relations—Fiction.
5. Journalism—Fiction.]   I. Title.
PZ7.Z3938Sw 2009   [Fic]—dc22   2008032024

ISBN 978-0-440-23859-1 (tr. pbk.)

Printed in the United States of America
10 9 8 7 6 5 4 3 2 1
First Trade Paperback Edition

For Cruce Stark—
my teacher, my mentor, my friend—
thank you, for everything.

Cooking a great meal is a little bit like falling in love. You can have the perfect recipe and the highest-quality ingredients in the exact amounts, but without that indefinable "something extra," it just doesn't work.

—*André Madison*

— 1 —

My boyfriend, Max, and I are lying on his twin bed, limbs tangled, foreheads pressed together, trying to catch our collective breath after a dizzying forty-five-minute make-out session, when he says the three most terrifying words in the English language:

"I love you."

Instinctively I recoil, my spine stiffening.

"Stella?" Max says, running his hand along the curve of my hip, pulling me back toward him. "Did you hear me?"

I mumble something along the lines of "mm-hmm" and try to paste on one of those mysterious Mona Lisa smiles.

Max scoots even closer and rolls slightly so that his mouth tickles the outside of my ear. "I said, 'I love you,' " he whispers throatily.

I respond the only way I know how: by pulling his face against mine and kissing him deeply.

Max isn't the first boy to tell me he loves me, but he is the first who seems to notice that I don't say it back. My best friend Kat would point out that this is because when most guys say "I love you," what they're really saying is "Let's get naked." She warned me about Max from the start. I thought he only asked me out because he was looking for a date to the junior prom, but Kat said I should be careful, because Max had never dated a girl for fewer than six months, not even freshman year.

That was almost nine weeks ago, and except for bringing me a single long-stemmed red rose on our "one-monthiversary," Max has kept the sentimental stuff to a minimum. This, frankly, is fine by me. I don't "do" mushy very well.

So before Max can make any more uncomfortable declarations, I tell him we need to get going.

"Mom needs me at the Kitchen," I remind him. "You can probably stay for dinner, if you want."

"Pass," he says. "I've got basketball with the guys tonight. But thanks for asking."

After planting one final kiss on the tip of my nose, Max scoots off the foot of the bed. He fishes his rumpled "Practice Safe Lunch—Use a Condiment" T-shirt off the floor, and I admire his tanned, toned chest as he pulls it over his head.

"You checkin' me out?" he asks.

I grin. "You know it."

"It doesn't seem fair," Max says. "You always take shirts while I play skins."

I do up the last three buttons on my top. "Good thing you're shooting hoops. You'll have plenty of time to work out some of that pent-up aggression."

Max groans, but in a playful way. It's one of the things I

like best about him. We're in our third month of dating, but so far he's let me set the pace in terms of fooling around. He doesn't give me crap about it, either. He drops hints here and there, and I usually have to redirect his hands once or twice, but there's no real pressure to do anything I don't want to do. Which is almost the exact opposite of my last boyfriend, Brice, who was never truly satisfied unless I let him knead one of my boobs or fondle the elastic of my underwear.

There are a lot of things I like about Max, though, that have nothing to do with Brice or any other guy I've ever dated. Like how he always opens the car door for me and waits until I'm tucked into my seat before closing it. Or how he lets me listen to WXPN when we're driving around, despite the fact that he can't stand most indie music. I like, too, that he calls me to touch base once a day—no more, no less—and doesn't mind when I make plans with my girlfriends for a Saturday night, even though I never bother to check with him first.

We don't talk much on the drive from Max's house to the Kitchen, which is another thing I like about him. He doesn't feel the need to fill the silence with a lot of meaningless chatter. I reach over and squeeze his knee in appreciation. He turns toward me and smiles, and it feels nice to know I've made him happy in some small way, even if I couldn't return the "I love you."

Max eases his VW Jetta into the parking lot of the shopping mall where the Open Kitchen is located. Before I get out I say, "So I'll see you tomorrow?"

"What's tomorrow?"

"Tuesday. Omar's party?" School has been out a little more than a week, but the never-ending string of summer parties is only just beginning.

Max shakes his head. "I totally forgot—I told Cory I'd take him to the Phillies game. But I can reschedule, if you want me to."

"No, no," I say. "Go with Cory."

"You won't be mad?"

"How can I be mad at a guy who's blowing me off to take his little brother to a ball game? Could you *be* more adorable?"

Max leans in for another kiss, and I relax into the warm saltiness of his mouth. When we break apart, I let my head lean against his shoulder for a second, and that's when he says it again:

"I really do love you, Stella."

On autopilot, I launch into Diversionary Tactic #2: rubbing my nose gently against the back of his ear and dropping a light kiss on the side of his neck. "And I," I say in my best sexy-girl voice, "really do love the way you smell."

Then I grab my bag and make a quick exit before he can say anything else.

I don't make it more than four steps toward the Kitchen when Enrique pops out of nowhere, puts his hand on my elbow, and steers me in the opposite direction.

"And hello to you, too," I say.

"Just . . . shhh."

We head into the English tearoom located on the end

of the strip. Enrique ushers me in and pulls me toward the display of Cadbury chocolates.

"What's with the cloak-and-dagger routine?" I ask. "Do you have some kind of top-secret hankering for a Fruit and Nut bar?"

Enrique rolls his eyes. This is something he does often. So often that he's turned the act of eye rolling into an art form.

"What?" I say, my voice sliding into a whine. "What is it?"

After a dramatic pause, he says, "I need to prepare you." His voice is grave and his face dead serious.

"Prepare me for what?"

Another dramatic pause, this one delivered with his eyes closed and accompanied by a deep intake of breath.

"Your mother hired the new intern today," he says finally.

"And . . . ?"

"And he is . . ."

"What? What is he?"

Enrique runs his meaty hands down the front of his blindingly white chef's coat and lets his breath out slowly. "*Stunning,*" he says finally.

I respond by punching him on the arm.

"Ow!" he cries. "What did you do that for?"

"To teach you a lesson."

"In what? Pain management?"

Ignoring him, I say, "Can we go now?"

"Actually, I was heading over here to buy a scone. You want one?"

I punch him again.

Enrique is a business partner of my mother's, as well as a certified drama queen. He's beefy, balding, and bordering on forty. He's also overwhelmingly devoted to a teacup Maltese named Miss Sugar, which he dresses in little doggie outfits worthy of *La Cage Aux Folles*.

As we wait for Enrique's scone, he says, "Don't you want to know *why* I think he's spectacular?"

"Not especially," I say. "I'm guessing it has something to do with him having a pulse?"

He purses his lips. "Fine. Be that way."

"Petulance is so last year," I say, thinking it will make him laugh. Instead, his scowl deepens. So I go, "Yay! A boy toy for you to drool over. I'm beyond enthused. Really."

"Not for me," Enrique protests. "For you. For *you* to drool over."

"Ah, so he's straight."

"As an arrow."

"Doesn't matter," I say. "I'm with Max, remember?"

"We're talking about *drooling*, babygirl. Not dating. And before you dismiss the idea, I should tell you that Intern Boy makes that Cavanaugh kid look like a prepubescent troll."

"Please do not refer to my boyfriend as a troll, thank you very much."

Enrique pays for his pastry and we head back to the Kitchen.

"So does this drool-worthy Intern Boy have a name?" I ask.

"Jeremy."

"And how old is Jeremy the Intern Boy?"

"He's in his second year at the Restaurant School, so he's got to be at least . . . what? Nineteen? Maybe twenty?"

Even if I weren't with Max—which I am (for now, anyway)—there's no chance my mother would let me date one of her employees. Especially not one so close to the legal drinking age, regardless of the fact that I turn eighteen in less than two weeks. So it really doesn't matter how drool-worthy Intern Boy may or may not be—he's off-limits.

Max. Thinking about him sends a panicked flutter through my chest. Why did he have to drop the L-bomb? We were having such a good time.

I sigh and follow Enrique into the Open Kitchen, which is the "restaurant school and interactive dining experience" my mom started almost two years ago. Basically, the place looks like the set of a cooking show on the Food Network, only our "audience" sits at café-height tables and gets to eat everything the master chef prepares. The chefs themselves come to Wilmington from all over the Delaware tristate area—big guns from Philly and Ocean City. We even get a few from New York once in a while. They promote their restaurants in exchange for providing gourmet four-course meals to our customers.

In addition to our "celebrity" chefs, we have Enrique, who's our house chef. He cooks on all the nights we don't have visiting chefs, plus every Sunday, when he hosts "Dinner at Five," which features retro favorites like beef Wellington with tomato aspic (read: gross vegetable Jell-O) and Baked Alaska for dessert. And this spring we had Bree, our first intern from the Restaurant School in Philadelphia, who took reservations, washed dishes, and served as prep cook whenever one was needed. She was twenty-one and had purple hair, two nose rings, and a vintage denim jacket signed by Sid Vicious. When I asked her who he was, she snorted seltzer through her nose, and the next day she handed me a burned CD of Sid's band, the Sex Pistols. Bree then appointed herself director of my musical education, and by the time she hung up her apron last month, she'd gotten me hooked on everyone from Tim Buckley to Interpol, this alt-rock band that has a song with my name in the title.

Standing behind the marble-topped island that comprises most of the Open Kitchen's "stage" is a very tall, very *solid* guy who I can only assume is Jeremy the Intern Boy. He's wearing regulation chef's whites and a red cowprint bandana that keeps thick, dark, McDreamy-from-*Grey's Anatomy* curls off his forehead. He looks up, and I'm surprised to see how . . . well . . . *manly* his face is. There's ruggedness to Jeremy's jawline, which is shaded with the kind of stubble that only heredity provides (as opposed to one of those electric razors with the K-Fed setting). His large, dark eyes flash brightly, and a sincere version of a TV-talk-show-host smile spreads across his plump lips.

"You must be Stella," he says in a voice like hot chocolate.

"Close your mouth, babygirl," Enrique whispers to me. "You're starting to drool."

— 2 —

THE OPEN KITCHEN
MENU FOR MONDAY, JUNE 15
Chef Paul Bonaventure of the Greenhouse
"Saluting Summer"
Strawberry and bleu cheese salad with white balsamic vinaigrette;
herbed sweet-potato chips with crème fraîche; chicken breasts
stuffed with roasted peaches and topped with a light Gorgonzola
cheese sauce; blueberry shortcake surprise

Chef Paul is demonstrating the proper way to pit a peach as my mother and Enrique clear the salad plates from the first course. I'm sitting at the computer, pretending to update our mailing list but really trying to sneak glances at Intern Boy as he loads the dishwasher. Enrique was right—Jeremy is totally drool-worthy. Of course, even evaluating the drool-worthiness of another guy makes me feel like I'm cheating on Max. *Must not absorb Jeremy's hotness*, I tell myself. *Must make self immune.*

I catch Enrique smirking at me from across the room, so I whip my head back toward the computer monitor and start clicking my fingers over the keyboard. The screen fills up with a bunch of gibberish, because I'm not actually typing anything. Then, feeling even more foolish than I do from getting caught scoping out Jeremy, I highlight the string of gibberish and press Delete.

How is it possible that Chef Paul hasn't even started preparing the main course?

Jeremy is loading freshly scrubbed sweet potatoes into the heavy silver mandolin—the food slicer, not the string instrument of the same name. It's one of my dad's favorite kitchen gadgets, though if he heard me call it a "gadget" he'd be appalled. ("They are tools, Stella," he's chastised me on more than one occasion. "Instruments of craft. Not . . . *gadgets.*") I find myself staring at Jeremy's hands as he begins to create a pile of paper-thin chips. Then my Spidey senses detect more smirking from Enrique, so I turn my attention to the computer again.

My legs start tingling like they do when I've had too much coffee and/or sugar, so I turn off the monitor, grab my cell phone, and slip out the front door to call Kat.

"Slow down," Kat commands, after I've filled her in on my angst-ridden day. "Who is this Jeremy and why do you keep talking about drool?"

"Forget about that part," I say. "The real question is, what am I going to do about Max?"

"You'll do what you always do: get spooked and continue to withdraw until the boy gets fed up and cuts you loose."

This is what Kat calls the Principle of Implosion. Her theory is that I'm too chicken to be in a real relationship but too much of a people-pleaser to break up with anyone. Instead, she says, I turn into Passive, Inaccessible Girlfriend until whoever I'm with gets the hint and dumps me. That way, I can claim I'm not directly responsible for the destruction of said relationship, even though I am.

I've never admitted this to anyone—especially not to Kat—but sometimes I think she might be right.

"What if I don't want to get spooked?" I say. "I think I might really like this guy. Like, *really* like him."

"Huh."

"*Huh?*" My voice jumps a couple of octaves. "All you can say is *huh?*"

"You know, I always figured you'd eventually find a boy who would make you want to be a girlfriend. I just never thought that boy would be Max Cavanaugh."

"What's wrong with Max?"

"Nothing's wrong with him," she says. "But he's . . . you know . . . *conventional*. And you, my dear, are anything but."

"Conventional?" I echo. "What do you mean by that?"

"He's, like, the quintessential boyfriend. He's cute, has lots of friends, gets decent grades, is athletic without being a jock. He's very . . . conventional."

Max is a textbook Capricorn—modest, hardworking, responsible—whereas Kat is a classic Leo—proud, colorful, fiercely independent. So it doesn't surprise me that she'd dub Max "conventional." I, on the other hand, was born a Cancer, and appropriately find myself torn between logic and emotion. Kind of like Spock from *Star Trek*, but with better-groomed eyebrows. This is probably why I find Max's Capricorn tendencies cute instead of annoying.

"Well, so what if he is conventional?" I say at last. "Maybe I *like* conventional."

"Maybe you do."

"I like Max," I say softly.

"So I've heard," she quips, and I can hear the smile in her voice. Then she says, "Come over tomorrow. Livvy can give you a ride."

The offer of transportation is crucial, as I am currently without a car and can only borrow Mom's when she's not working at the Kitchen (translation: next to never). In fact, this is something Mom and I argue about regularly. I've logged countless hours at the Kitchen since we first opened, and I've diligently banked a minimum of half my weekly wages in hopes that I will one day be able to afford a Consumer Reports–rated certified used car. The thing is, I get paid so little that even with my stringent savings plan, I'm still about fifteen hundred dollars short. It's frustrating, because I could've easily bought a beater at the end of last summer, but none passed Mom's inspection. So I continue to slave away for a pittance, and my social life remains at the mercy of my friends and/or current boyfriend.

"Tomorrow, okay?" Kat repeats. "I promise the three of us will spend at least twenty minutes dissecting your relationship with Max Cavanaugh, okay?"

"Ha, ha."

"See you then!"

Back in the Kitchen, Jeremy and Chef Paul are trussing up the peach-stuffed chickens. Mom's drying wineglasses by hand; she looks at me, one eyebrow arched, as if to say, "Everything okay?" I answer her silent question with a reassuring wave. She nods: message received.

Even if Mom wasn't in the middle of a dinner, I

wouldn't talk to her about what Max said. And I certainly wouldn't tell her that I think the new intern is beyond breathtaking. We don't do that kind of girl talk. We've never done it. I've had crushes on boys since kindergarten—once I was kicked out of an elementary school production of *Peter Pan* after Nathan Schroeder and I got caught "making out" behind the stuffed Saint Bernard that served as Nana—but even then, the only reason Mom found out about Nathan was because the guidance counselor called her to discuss my "problem with inappropriate physical contact." Ironic, considering that Nathan and I thought that making out consisted of holding hands and trading kisses on the cheek. But whatever.

Needing distraction, I queue up my "Bootyshaking" playlist on iTunes, slip on some noise-reducing headphones, and get back to work.

The kitchen timer dings and Kat calls out, "Turn!" On her command, the three of us—Kat, Olivia, and me—roll onto our backs. It's eighty-six degrees and we've been hanging out at Kat's house all morning, as hers is the one with the inground pool, split-level deck, and supercushy lounge chairs. The sun sizzles against my marginally SPF-protected skin. I'm looking forward to soaking up enough rays to produce a warm, golden glow of a tan.

"Stella, what's with the suit?" Kat asks out of nowhere.

I shield my eyes with one hand and squint in her direction. "What do you mean?"

"The straps on your halter," she says. "Think of the tan line."

I sit up and try to survey my lime green bikini top. *Teen*

Vogue promised it would give a small-chested girl like me the illusion of a bigger bust, while the navy blue boy-short bottoms would slim out my bum and thighs.

"Don't get me wrong," Kat continues. "It's great for a pool party. You should totally wear it to Omar's tonight. But how do you expect to look good in a cami this summer if you've got some geometric pale-skin pattern crossing your shoulders and neck? Trailer park, anyone?"

"Leave her alone," Olivia mumbles from the next chair over, her voice thick with sleep.

"So what do you suggest I do about this fashion tragedy?" I ask Kat, amused.

"At least undo the *straps*," Kat whines.

Livvy shakes her head and says, "Girl, give it a rest." Then she swings up off her chaise, strides toward the pool, and dives right in without another word.

Kat flicks her Gucci sunglasses from faux-headband position back over her eyes. "*Someone's* PMS-ing."

I look over at Kat, stretched out like a *Sports Illustrated* swimsuit model, one freakishly long leg bent at an artful angle. *Her* bikini consists of four crocheted triangles and a lot of strings—an original Kat O'Connor design, no less. Everything about Kat is long and lean, from her neck to her toes. She looks sort of catlike, actually, with her big green eyes and sleek black hair. Kat's slinky in the way she moves, too; when she walks, it looks like she's hearing some kind of smoky jazz playing in her head.

Olivia, on the other hand, looks like her body was built using a series of sharp chisels. Her face could be a geometry assignment unto itself. The only exception is her kinky-curly hair, which she stopped having chemically straightened two years ago ("It's the classic symbol of black female oppression," she explained). So now Liv has these tight black coils about an inch long sprouting from her scalp.

And then there's me, Stella Madison. The only offspring of André and Amy Madison, who would be—should be?—celebrating their twenty-year anniversary on August 14, exactly eight weeks and three days from today. I'm neither tall nor short, neither fat nor skinny, neither ugly nor beautiful. I have a lot of medium brown hair that hangs halfway down my back in semitwisty curls, and violet eyes ("Elizabeth Taylor's eyes," my dad always calls them) that are sort of pretty but way too big for the rest of my face, which is on the small side and what beauty magazines call heart-shaped. Fortunately I inherited my father's good skin and my mother's perfect teeth, so all in all, I think I got a pretty good deal in the looks department.

Tonight's my father's monthly appearance at the Open Kitchen. He's a world-renowned chef, albeit a reluctant one. It's hard for me to understand, since he's always been just my dad. But apparently his commitment to classic cuisine has made him a sort of antihero across several continents. While the other guys are monkeying around in molecular gastronomy, which is this mad-scientist way of cooking, my dad's all about the French tradition. His latest venture, Mélange, is a four-star upscale eatery in the Old City neighborhood of Philadelphia that specializes in French and Northern Italian haute cuisine. But it's not so much the style of the food that's the draw as it is the method by which it's made. Dad believes in purity when it comes to ingredients, and he and his staff make almost everything from scratch, including stuffing their own sausage and cultivating their own cheeses. So while he's not instantly recognizable, like Jacques Pépin or Emeril Lagasse, the mere mention of his name inspires reverence among chefs and foodies alike.

Summers are slow for us at the Kitchen, so even though Dad's cooking tonight, there are still a few seats to be filled. Sometimes Mom lets me invite Kat and Liv before she offers the slots (gratis) to her favorite repeat customers, and they almost always accept—especially when my dad is on. He can be so charming. He's always asking Olivia to read him some of her poetry. Liv is brilliant and writes this edgy women-rawk stuff she performs at coffeehouses and slam competitions. Or he'll notice a piece of jewelry Kat's wearing that she made herself and tell her how fabulous it is. My dad's the only guy who can make Kat blush, and it's a consistent reaction. I think she's got a bit of a crush on him, actually.

"It's that thick French accent," Liv says. "Hell, it almost makes *me* hot."

Neither Kat nor Olivia fully understands why my parents broke up. This is not surprising. Technically, my family is fractured, but you wouldn't know it from watching my mom and dad interact. Which is rather often, considering that they've been legally separated for nearly six years. My mom still keeps the books for him at his restaurant. She says that's why they haven't bothered to get an official divorce—their finances are too complicated, too "intertwined"—but I know the real reason.

It's because they never fell out of love.

Unfortunately, in real life, love doesn't carry the same currency as it does in the movies. In real life, two people who love each other can still end up apart.

The oven timer dings again, but instead of shouting "Turn," Kat says, "I think it's time for a dip. Coming?"

"I'll be there in a minute," I say. I need time to weigh the benefits of cool water on hot skin versus the havoc the pool's chlorine will wreak on my curls.

My hair, it should be noted, is like a barometer. If I wake up and see Brillo-esque curls forming around my face, then I'm about ninety percent certain that it will rain in the next twenty-four hours. If I wake up and see glamour-girl waves, I know it's safe to wear short sleeves and bring a sweater. I'm totally serious. Even my mom looks at my hair before deciding on an outfit.

Then I see Kat do a graceful dolphin-like dive into the deep end, and watch Olivia freestyle her umpteenth lap, and my mind is made up. I'll simply have to slip in a hot-oil treatment before dinner.

"Look out!" I call. I sprint across the deck and pop a cannonball, then splash into the bracing cold water.

Bliss.

Around four o'clock, we girls part ways to shower and change. I don't normally get dressed up for dinner at the Kitchen—beyond looking clean and presentable, that is— but I do take special care on the nights my dad cooks. And since we're heading to Omar's afterward, I not only apply that hot-oil treatment, but also slather on a white-clay facial mask, rub shimmering body lotion on every square inch of skin, and paint my toenails a particularly fetching shade of raspberry.

I've just finished a second coat on my nails when the phone rings. Such timing! My face is imprisoned beneath the thick, bone-dry mask I applied almost forty minutes ago—the kind that flakes off in powdery chunks if you breathe too hard. I would let the machine get it if I weren't the kind of person who checks e-mail seventeen times a day and gets depressed on postal holidays.

So I swoop up the cordless and mumble hello, trying not to crack the mask too terribly.

"Hello," a deep male voice says into my ear. "Is Stella Madison available?"

"This is she," I say, but the muffled words sound more like "Ish i shee."

There's a pause, and I don't know if it's because the caller can't understand what I said or because the phone got cut off or what.

Screw the mask. I yawn on purpose, freeing my skin from the tight clay. "I'm Stella," I say. "This is her. She. Her?"

"She," the guy says, and laughs. "You had it right the first time."

This is not a voice I recognize. For a second I wonder if it might be Jeremy the Intern Boy—but only for a second.

"Stella, this is Mike Hardwick over at the *Daily Journal*."

"Oh," I say. "We already have a subscription."

He laughs again. "I'm not trying to sell you something, Stella. Actually, I'm calling because there's an unexpected opening in our internship program, and your journalism teacher, Ms. Duke, thought you might be interested. She sent me some of your clips, and I have to say, I was impressed."

Didn't see this one coming.

"Wow," I say. "Really?"

"Each summer the *Journal* offers temporary paid positions to aspiring journalists. Mostly college students, but we always reserve one slot for a promising high school writer."

"And that's . . . me?"

"Sort of," Mike says. "Typically interns need to apply for the position. But the gal we hired for this year had a family emergency and is spending the bulk of the summer out of state. We spoke to a few other applicants, but at this late date, most have made alternate arrangements."

Ah. This makes more sense. Even though I finished the year with an A in journalism, I only took the class because of a scheduling error. Ms. Duke was superencouraging—especially when we were working on feature stories, as opposed to dry news stuff—but still, I don't even *read* the newspaper, let alone dream of writing for one.

"You've got a fresh voice, Stella, and we'd like to put it to work. Think you might be interested?"

"Um," I say. "I don't know. What would I be doing?"

"Well, I won't lie. You'll be doing a lot of grunt work—typing in wedding announcements and obits, updating the dining guide, stuff like that. But we also have something kind of special in mind for you. I'd love to have you come down to the office and talk more about it."

I hesitate, mostly because I know Mom's expecting me to work nights at the Kitchen. I'm pretty sure juggling two jobs would leave very little time to have any kind of social life.

"It pays three hundred a week," Mike adds.

Nothing like money to motivate a girl. I quickly do the math; if I took the gig, I'd have enough money to get a Mom-approved car before the start of senior year.

"Sure," I say quickly. "I'm definitely interested."

"Great!" Mike says. "Think you can come in tomorrow?"

We agree to meet at the *Journal* office at eleven the next day. I grin as I put the phone back in its charger, not caring about the major mask crackage. This could turn out to be really cool. Not only is the money sweet, but an internship is just the kind of thing Mr. Carney, my guidance counselor, has been bugging me about so that I'll have something meaty for my college applications next year.

After I wash the last chunks of the mask off, I grab the phone and flop back onto my bed. Max answers on the third ring.

"Hey, you," he says, sounding warm and lazy, like a perfect summer day.

"Guess what?" I say. "I think I might have a job! A real one!"

I fill Max in on my conversation with Mike Hardwick. Max is duly impressed and offers to give me a ride to the interview.

"Really? You'd do that?"

"Of course," he says. "Why wouldn't I?"

We chat for a few more minutes before I realize that if I don't get my butt in gear, I'm going to be late for Kat and Livvy.

"Have fun tonight," I tell Max. "Eat a couple hot dogs for me, okay?"

"Will do."

Two things occur to me after Max and I say our good-byes: there was no further mention of the L-word (relief!), and I called Max about my good(ish) news even before I called Kat.

It's this second realization that whops the biggest impact. I always, always call Kat first about everything. The pecking order is Kat, Livvy, Mom, Dad, and *then* whatever boy I'm currently entangled with. Sometimes I don't even make it that far down the list.

Maybe Kat was right. Maybe Max *is* the kind of boy who makes me want to be a girlfriend. I haven't strapped on my running shoes . . . yet.

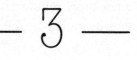

THE OPEN KITCHEN

MENU FOR TUESDAY, JUNE 16

Chef André Madison of Mélange

"A Night at the Bistro"

Mussels Provençal with roasted fennel and heirloom tomatoes;
Normandy-style onion soup topped with baked gruyère crouton;
Beef Bourguignon braised in red wine, onions, apple-wood-
smoked bacon, and mushrooms, with roasted-garlic whipped
potatoes; dark chocolate profiteroles with salted caramel ice cream

I take Kat's advice and wear my *Teen Vogue*–approved bikini under a white three-quarter-sleeved summer cardigan with pearl buttons and a new low-slung madras miniskirt that shows off my midriff quite nicely. Cork-heeled strappy sandals and a macramé purse Kat made me so I didn't have to buy the one I saw at Target complete the look. The hot-oil treatment I applied before I showered has turned my frizz-prone curls into soft, glossy waves. I slick on a bit of Smashbox lip gloss, brush on a quick coat of clear mascara, and rub some gold-flecked lotion into my sun-pinkened cheeks.

Not bad. Not bad at all.

"Hot mama alert!" Olivia says when she and Kat come to pick me up.

I grin. "Let's get out of here."

But Kat isn't moving. Her almond eyes narrow in my direction, and I see that her hands are resting on her hips. "I thought you said Max couldn't come."

"He can't. He's at a ball game."

"Then who's the dude?"

"Dude?" I echo.

"*Dude*," she says again. "You don't get all dolled up like this for no reason. Does this have anything to do with that Jeremy guy you were talking about yesterday?"

"Don't be silly," I say, flipping my hair over one shoulder. "It's a party. Am I not allowed to look nice for a party? Even if my very *conventional* boyfriend will not be in attendance?"

Kat remains unconvinced. "You're evading my question."

"Enough with the detective work, Nancy Drew," Olivia chimes in. "If we don't leave now, we'll be late to dinner."

Olivia's driving, so Kat takes shotgun, as her legs are too long to fold into the backseat of Liv's Ford Focus.

The two of them argue over radio stations while I sit quietly in the back, wondering why I don't want to say anything to the girls about tomorrow's interview. It's not that big a deal, really. If I get the job, then cool. If not, then . . . cool.

When we roll into the parking lot, it's almost full, not only because we're late but because there's a Weight

— 23 —

Watchers meeting raging next door. The women stare through the window as we climb out of the Focus, adjust our skirts, and scamper into the Kitchen.

"Stella!" my father's heavily French-accented voice booms across the room. "Come give your old papa a hug!"

"Hey, Dad," I say, feeling self-conscious as he wraps his big bear arms around me and picks me up high enough that my feet clear the floor. My dad gives Kat and Olivia equally enthusiastic greetings as I survey the room. Only a couple of new faces tonight. Mom's business relies heavily on two types of clientele: people who rent out the place for private parties, like all the corporate bigwigs from pharmaceutical companies, and repeat customers who come in once or twice a month. Despite the steep prices— dinner runs anywhere from fifty dollars per person to ninety, depending on how famous the chef is and what ingredients he or she decides to use—we do have a roster of couples who've become virtual fixtures. You get to know them pretty well after a while.

One face I recognize instantly is that of Masha Tobash, who's a thirtysomething programming director at the Food Network in New York. She takes the train down every couple of months when my dad's cooking, to try to convince him that he should have his own show. The network has been after him for years—at one point, Masha vowed to make him an Iron Chef—but my father has absolutely no desire to follow in the footsteps of guys like Bobby Flay or Emeril Lagasse.

"Emeril, he makes good food, is a great chef," my dad explained once. "But it's always 'Bam!' this and 'Bam!'

that. To make cooking a . . . a . . . *performance*—it is disre-
spectful to the food."

"Hypocritical much?" I asked. "Considering what you
do at the Kitchen and all."

"That's different," he said. "That is teaching."

"Isn't that what those guys on TV do?" I goaded him.
"Teach?"

He sighed heavily. "Cooking is a science. It is an art, a
craft. It does not work unless you give it your heart and
soul and sweat. How can you do this when you are worried about camera angles and the next commercial break?"

My father's aversion to having his own television show
is just another one of the reasons my parents separated.
My dad, although utterly brilliant in the kitchen, is bad at
business. And when I say bad, I mean *bad*. He designed Le
Nain, the first restaurant he owned, to celebrate authentic
French peasant food. After pouring most of his and
Mom's savings into the venture, he pretty much disappeared from our lives, spending close to twenty hours a
day, seven days a week trying to perfect its menu, the star
of which was his sausage cassoulet (a dish that is, essen-
tially, pork and beans).

Le Nain tanked about four months after it opened—
people weren't exactly thrilled with the idea of dropping
sixty bucks a head on such "rustic" fare—and the failure
nearly wrecked my normally resilient father. He was so
depressed that he spent two full weeks in bed, drinking a
quarter of his wine collection and ranting about how
Americans were too stupid to understand the "exquisite
beauty of simple foods."

Although Mélange has done much better than Le Nain, Dad still insists on closing it November through January every year. For at least two of those months he travels through Europe, spending most of the profits he hasn't put back into the business. Even then, almost all of his "mad money" goes toward ordering mass quantities of wine, which he then sells at the restaurant for maybe fifteen percent above cost. (Most restaurateurs jack up the price by at *least* forty.) Despite how Dad's always talking about taking me to Europe, I've never actually been outside of the States. There's always some perfectly reasonable-sounding excuse, like how my school breaks are too short for me to soak up the full experience, or how summers are too touristy, and besides, those are Dad's most lucrative months at Mélange, so how could he possibly take a vacation?

Sometimes I get the feeling that my father doesn't actually *want* me to go to Europe, even though we've got family over in France that I've never even met. Mom says this is because Dad has such mixed feelings about going back there himself.

"It's a love/hate thing," she says. "Your dad moved here when he was twenty-four, but he never intended to stay. This country was to him what France is to many American chefs—another training ground. But he became such a rock star on the East Coast, he just . . . stuck around. And then he met me, and we had you, and the rest you know."

My parents met when she was working as the office manager for this Italian place in Baltimore where my dad was head chef. Mom's always trying to help Dad improve his bottom line, suggesting cost-cutting measures or marketing ideas. But he's far too interested in new ways to cook Jerusalem artichokes to take any of her advice. Mom's frustration with his complete lack of interest in anything other than his "art and craft" is what inspired her to start the Open Kitchen in the first place.

"The difference between me and your father," she's said on more than one occasion, "is that he thinks great food should only be eaten by people who know what great food is all about. Me, I like to introduce people to new flavors, new textures, new ways of appreciating what they put into their mouths."

Funny how she never seems to appreciate what I like to put in *my* mouth. I mean, I know Whoppers aren't haute cuisine, but honestly, is there really anything better than a flame-broiled burger?

"Stella, love!" Masha calls out to me, rising from her chair. She throws her arms around me dramatically and kisses both cheeks, European style, even though I know she was born in Nutley, New Jersey. In fact, her real name is *Marsha*, not Masha, but she decided to change it in college because Marsha was too "pedestrian." She's got a habit of spilling deep personal secrets when she's had a little too much Vouvray.

"Hey, Masha," I say. "How've you been?"

"Meh," she says, rolling her eyes a bit. "I'd be better if you could figure out how I can convince your hardheaded father to take a meeting with my crew in New York."

"Good luck with that."

Masha turns her gaze to my dad, a mischievous smirk on her lips. Kat swears Masha's got the hots for my dad, but Olivia thinks that observation is more about Kat's jealousy than her intuition. Yet even Enrique, who tends to get bored by what he calls "hetero head games," thinks Masha's interest in my father goes beyond the culinary.

"Are you two talking about me again?" Dad calls over his shoulder as he washes his hands in the sink. I almost—*almost*—miss the nine-hundred-watt smile he flashes at Masha. At least, I think it was for Masha. It's not the same kind of smile he normally gives me. Too many teeth, too much twinkle in the eye.

Kat grabs my arm and pulls me away from Masha.

"Did you see that?" she whispers into my ear.

I nod.

"You think they're into something?" she asks.

"Like what?"

"Like . . ." Kat's voice trails off meaningfully. "You know."

"What? No. Uh-uh."

"How can you be so sure?"

"Because," I say indignantly. "He and my mom are still married, remember?"

Kat's look grows slightly worried. "But, Stella—it's been, like, five years, right?"

"Six."

"Six years," she repeats. "You honestly think your dad's not getting a little action somewhere?"

"Shut *up*!" I say, my voice a bit too loud. Then, more quietly: "That's my *father* you're talking about. I like to pretend my parents don't have sex lives, okay? It helps me sleep better at night."

Kat shakes her head. "So, what? You were the result of an immaculate conception?"

Thankfully, Olivia sidles up to us before any more can be said about procreation.

"Who's the hottie?" she asks.

I turn and see Jeremy coming in through the back entrance, holding two heavy plastic shopping bags.

"That's Jeremy," I say casually. "He's the new intern."

"*Hel*-lo," Kat purrs. "Definitely an improvement over that purple-haired chick."

I excuse myself and head over to say hi to my mom, who's been running credit cards since we walked through the door.

"What's with the last-minute shopping?" I ask.

"Your father," she says, "decided twenty minutes ago that he wasn't happy with the mushrooms. I told Jeremy to pick up whatever he could find that looked fresh—what a godsend that kid is! You know how picky Dad gets about produce. Hey, you're looking pretty spiffy tonight. Any reason?"

"Party," I say.

"Again?"

"Typical end-of-the-school-year circuit," I explain. "It'll die down soon."

Mom goes to greet two more late customers while I flip through the book to find out where the girls and I are sitting. She's put us at Masha's table, which could be a problem, considering Kat. But before I can even think about how to deal with that potential complication, I see Jeremy heading toward me.

"Hey there," he says, brushing my shoulder as he slips around me to get to the computer.

"Hey," I say back. "Need any help?"

"You got some Valium stashed in your pocket?" he deadpans. "I swear, I feel like a fourteen-year-old girl at her first prom."

"Um, why?"

He smiles sheepishly. "I'm a huge fan of your father," he confesses. "It's like being in the presence of royalty, you know? I keep making these stupid newbie mistakes. Nerves, I guess."

"Oh, god," I groan. "Not another groupie."

Jeremy tilts his head to one side. "What's that?"

"Nothing," I say. "Shouldn't you be, like, chopping mushrooms or something?" I try to sound like I'm teasing, but my voice comes out sharper than intended.

"Yes, ma'am," he replies. His tone is clipped, like I'm his drill sergeant. Before I can apologize he's back behind the island with my dad.

The girls have already planted themselves at Masha's table, Kat directly across from her (to keep tabs, I presume) and Olivia to her right. They're discussing the menu when I slip into my seat.

"I don't do mussels," Kat declares.

"Then you're missing out," Masha says, and takes a swig of wine.

Kat glares at Masha. I send Olivia a silent SOS with my eyes, and she nods slightly.

"So, Masha," Olivia says, "what's new at the network? Anything you can dish about? No pun intended."

I smile gratefully at Olivia. She lifts her water glass as if to say, "No problem."

For the next fifteen minutes or so, Masha prattles on about her job. I watch Jeremy build a cheese and fruit platter for each table; when he delivers ours, he seems to purposely avoid making eye contact with me. Then again, I could be projecting. I pick some black grapes out from under an oozing triangle of Brie, wondering why I even care.

Dinner goes smoothly, despite Masha's determination to get sauced. By the time dessert is served, the waistband of my skirt feels snug. I take two bites and pass the rest to Olivia, who's got the metabolism of a hummingbird. She eats more than Kat and me combined, but her body is all sinew and muscle. Go figure.

People begin to leave, full and tipsy and happy. I stand up from my bar-height chair and stretch. Then, out of general politeness, I ask Masha if she needs a ride to the train station.

Her face flushes a deeper shade of pink and she stammers something about not wanting to be a burden.

"We're heading in that direction," I tell her. "So it's no problem, really."

"Stella, I'm fine," she snaps. Then, in a gentler tone, she says, "Thank you anyway." She excuses herself and heads toward the ladies' room.

"Damn, girl," Olivia says, when Masha's out of earshot. "What crawled up her pantyhose and died?"

I shrug. "Where's Kat?"

"Trying to talk the new boy into going to Omar's with us."

I scan the room, and sure enough, Kat's pressed up against Jeremy in the narrow pantry.

"She's wasting her time," I say. "He's, like, nineteen or something."

"So?" Olivia counters.

"So he's not going to want to hang out with a bunch of high school kids."

"I don't know," Liv says. "He seems to be enjoying Kit-Kat's company."

"Whatever."

My dad pours himself a glass of red, swirls it a few times, and takes a nice big mouthful. Then he saunters over to me.

"Not my best meal, eh?" he asks. "Too heavy for the weather, I think."

I shrug. "Meat and potatoes are much more my speed than some of that other stuff you like to torture me with."

Dad throws his left hand across his heart dramatically. "You kill me when you talk like that! How can you, the only child of my loins, say such things?"

It's a rhetorical question, one I've heard over and over and over. It gets old, actually. I don't know why my parents can't accept the fact that I'm not and never will be a foodie. It doesn't make me any less their daughter just because I prefer chicken nuggets to squab (which is really just a fancy name for pigeon, by the way).

"Dad, I have to go," I say. "The girls and I have plans."

He takes another gulp of wine. "Of course you do. You're young! You're beautiful! You have many boys' hearts to break!"

His words are cheesy but the sentiment is sweet. I give him an impulsive hug. "Are we still on for Thursday?"

"Yes, yes, of course."

"And you're sure you won't be too busy?"

Dad gives my nose a playful pinch. "I am never too busy for my Stella-belle."

I look around for my mother, to kiss her goodnight, and see she's been cornered by Mrs. Abruggio, one of the white-haired regulars, who in her early years as a wife and mother took many, many cooking classes. She fancies herself some kind of five-star home chef and likes to deconstruct each meal at the Kitchen with whoever she can get to listen.

I turn to Dad and say, "Be a hero and go rescue Mom from Mrs. Abruggio. And tell her I said goodnight—Mom, I mean, not Mrs. A."

Dad rolls his eyes—he's been caught in the clutches of Mrs. Abruggio far too many times—but after downing the rest of his wine and refilling his glass, he heads over, booming, "Mrs. Abruggio, why have you not come to say hello? I thought I was your favorite. . . ."

Kat emerges from the pantry, a nice pink flush in her cheeks. "All set?"

I turn to Olivia. "Told you."

"Told her what?" Kat asks.

"That Jeremy wouldn't want to hang at some high school party."

"Wrong," Kat says. "Here he comes now."

It's the first time I've seen Jeremy out of his kitchen scrubs. He's wearing a butter yellow V-neck T-shirt that not only shows off his deeply tanned skin but also reveals just a touch of dark, curly chest hair. I involuntarily suck air through my teeth.

"Ladies," he says, punctuating the word with a slow, sexy grin. "Give me five and I'll be ready to roll."

"You should've asked me," I hiss at Kat, when Jeremy's out of earshot.

"Asked you what?"

"If it was okay to invite him."

Kat's eyes narrow. "Why wouldn't it be okay? I thought Max wasn't the jealous type."

"He's not," I say. "It's just . . . well, *hi*, Jeremy works for my mom, remember?"

"So?" Kat says with a shrug. "It's not like you drink or smoke or anything. What can he rat you out for? Having fun?"

I turn to Liv for support, but I can tell this is one battle she doesn't feel like fighting.

"Fine," I say. "Whatever."

We head out to the car; Jeremy follows a few minutes later. I climb into my usual seat, which puts Jeremy in the back with me, much to Kat's dismay. I take a perverse pleasure in this.

"Put your seat belt on," Jeremy instructs. "Oh, and your mom told me to tell you that you don't have to be home until two."

"In the morning?" I ask, incredulous.

"I promised to keep you safe," he says. Then Jeremy leans in close—close enough that I can feel his breath hot on my neck—and says, "You in that skirt? You're going to *need* my protection tonight."

My breath catches in my throat, and when Jeremy sinks back into his seat I have to fight the urge to grab his T-shirt and pull him against my aching chest.

I have a boyfriend, I tell myself. *I have a boyfriend.*

"Everything okay back there?" Kat asks, angling her mirror to meet my gaze.

"Fine," I croak.

"Then let's roll."

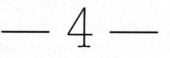

— 4 —

We arrive at Omar's around ten. His house is on the edge of Newark, a four-bedroom Colonial with the most amazing backyard. Not quite as posh as Kat's, but infinitely earthier and more sensual. Garden beds dot the perimeter, each one filled with fragrant things like lavender and freesia and sweet jasmine. Tiny Chinese paper lanterns crisscross the deck's lattice "roof," and there are flaming tikki torches smelling of citronella tied at intervals to the railing. There's a copper fire pit set in the middle of the cedar deck, around which a bunch of newly graduated girls in short-shorts are perched on their boyfriends' laps, all of them roasting marshmallows and feeding the gooey balls of sugar to each other. To the extreme left sits a large, soft-sided hot tub crammed with beautiful people sucking down fruity-looking drinks decorated with those cheesy umbrellas on toothpicks.

In other words, it's paradise.

Liv ditches us almost immediately, making a beeline for the outdoor bar, which Omar is manning. Liv's the reason we were invited to this party to begin with; she and Omar have been engaging in a *will they?/won't they?*

flirtation for the last half of the school year. It was mostly *won't they?* until about three weeks ago, when Omar broke up with Kendra, his sophomore girlfriend, who was infected with a major case of the green-eyed monster. (Not that this was entirely unwarranted, as Omar is something of a player and had been doing some hard-core flirting with Liv for nearly three months. And that's just one documented case of Omar's wandering eye.)

Kat's strategy is far more direct. She strips off her second-skin tank top to reveal a variation of the crocheted bikini she was wearing earlier today, links her arm through Jeremy's, and says, "Let's check out the pool, 'kay?" It puts me in the awkward position of having to decide whether to follow them (third wheel) or stay behind (loser with no friends). Before I can actually *make* a decision, they're off.

I scan the scene, desperate to locate some friendly faces. This is literally the eighth party we've been to since school let out, yet everyone looks like a stranger to me. My left hand feels light and empty, and I want to smack myself when I realize this is because I've grown sort of used to having Max's fingers entwined with mine.

I dig through my purse and pull out my teal blue Sidekick. Max won't care if I call him. The ball game should be ending soon anyway. I bring up my contact list and highlight "Max Cell" but flip the phone closed before I actually dial. I won't—I *can't*—be that girl.

Just when I'm thinking it would be impossible to feel

any more lost, Liv surprises me from behind and hands me one of those fruity drinks the girls in the hot tub were slurping down.

"Oh, my god," she says, sounding like disco lights and glitter. "You have to taste. So good."

"What's in it?"

Liv shrugs. "Fruit, ice, maybe a little rum. I watched Omar make them myself, so I can assure you that nobody slipped anything scary into the mix."

I nod. This is why I don't normally drink at parties. It's not that I'm a goody-goody—Dad's been giving me wine practically since I was teething—but you read all these horror stories about what happens to girls who aren't vigilant about babysitting their red plastic cups. It always seems easier to abstain.

Tonight, though, I'm feeling like it might not be such a bad thing to get a little buzz going. I take a tentative sip and am surprised by the sweet, syrupy coconut taste that fills my mouth.

"Good, huh?" Liv says, downing half her drink in one long gulp. Livvy made the decision for me; I'm done for the night. I hand her my drink back and extend the other empty palm.

"Keys, please?"

Liv nods and hands them over. "Thanks for being such a Girl Scout." She plants a wet, coconutty kiss on my cheek and bounces back over to Omar before I can say another word.

Alone again, naturally.

With nothing to do and no one to talk to, my eyes

home in on the pool area. Target: Kat and Jeremy. Kat's still got one hand on Jeremy's arm. His back is to me, so I can't see his reaction, but I can see hers. She's looking up at him, smiling coyly. Then *her* eyes cut away and laser in on me.

Kat arches one eyebrow, and without breaking her gaze, the hand not touching Jeremy's arm reaches up and brushes a lock of hair from his face. I feel myself wince involuntarily, but I can't figure out if it's because Kat's showing off for my benefit or because . . . well, I can't even think of the other option. I shut my eyes and silently chant Max's name: *Max, Max, Max, I'm with Max.*

I'm trying to screw my head on straight when this soccer stud thumps my upper arm with his elbow. He's carrying six tall shooters of something creamy, three in each hand, and to me he says, "Brain Damage?"

At first I think maybe he's referring to the band that's playing over the stellar speaker system, but then he says, "Come on, try a shot."

"No thanks."

"What's the matter?" he taunts. "Afraid of playing with the grown-ups?"

"There are grown-ups here?" I say, looking around. "Where?"

I turn in time to see Kat striding toward me, sans Jeremy. "Not interested!" she trills. Then she grabs my arm and pulls me inside the glass door to Omar's house, locking it behind us.

"Thanks for the rescue."

Kat nods. "That guy's a tool. He's got this girl-friend who goes to New Castle Baptist, but whenever she's not around he macks on anything with a pulse. No offense."

"None taken."

Kat fiddles with the hem of her tank top, which I now notice is back on over the crocheted bikini. "So, Stella," she says, "why did you lie to me?"

"Huh?"

"*Jeremy,*" she says, her green eyes bright and hard. "It's so obvious that you're into him."

"Am not," I say, but there's a definite lack of conviction in my voice. Even I can hear it.

Kat points a peony-painted fingernail in my direction and says, "*J'accuse!*"

It's hard for me to lie to my girlfriends, especially Kat, who's sharper than a brand-new Santoku knife. And normally I don't have a reason to lie, so it's no big deal. But Kat's already been dogging my relationship with Max, and if I admit that okay, yes, I am finding myself drawn to Intern Boy, she's going to turn into the poster girl for the Dump Max Express.

So I deflect.

"You should go check on Liv," I say. "She's downing fruity rum drinks like they're water. I took her keys already, but someone should make sure she doesn't . . . you know . . ."

"Let the booze evaporate her morals," Kat finishes for me. "Right. Got it covered."

She turns to walk away and then stops. "Speaking of covered . . . why don't *you* go check on Jeremy? I saw Lori

Pfefferminz eyeing him earlier, and I know you wouldn't want *her* to dig her acrylic claws into him on your watch."

The smirk that appears on her face is beyond infuriating, but I hold my tongue.

After Kat goes to babysit Olivia, I count to one hundred in my head. Then I do exactly what she told me I should do: go find Jeremy. He's in the far back end of the yard, sitting on a wooden bench swing suspended from a massive oak tree, balancing a bottle of Yuengling on one knee and staring blankly into the distance. I slip into the spot next to him.

"Hey there," I say.

"Hey," he says back.

"Nice night, huh?"

Jeremy smiles. "Yeah. Nice."

"So whatcha looking at?"

He points out a group of junior boys, clad in the familiar uniform of baggy khaki shorts and cotton polo shirts, who've formed a Hacky Sack circle in the middle of the yard.

"Forget for a second that Hacky Sack is unquestionably so ten years ago," he says. "Do you recognize the absolute beauty in this ritual display of teenage male prowess? It's like *Mutual of Omaha's Wild Suburban Kingdom* out there."

He laughs, and it is a sound as smooth and rich as a triple-thick black-and-white malted from the Charcoal Pit. I shiver, and the blush in my cheeks intensifies.

"See that guy over there, the blond one in the blue shirt, with the collar slightly popped?"

"Yeah."

"Now, scan over to his two o'clock, to that Jessica Alba look-alike dancing with her girlfriends. She's been eyeing him for at least twenty minutes, fiddling with the spaghetti straps on her top. He hasn't checked her out once, but if you notice the practiced nonchalant expression on his face, you can tell that he knows someone's watching.

"Okay, and now look! See what she's doing?"

The girl plucks the paper umbrella from her friend's drink and tucks it behind one ear. Her eyes dart over to Popped Collar Guy, then just as quickly cut away.

"Classic plumage," Jeremy continues. "She's screaming, 'Look at me! Look at me!' "

Now it's my turn to laugh. "Someone's been watching a little too much *Meerkat Manor*, hasn't he?"

"Oh, man," he says. "The meerkats. Who doesn't love the meerkats?"

Jeremy smiles at me again, a slow, sleepy smile. He leans back into the swing, stretching one arm across the back. If I wasn't sitting so close to the end of the seat, his arm would be around *me*.

"So . . . ," I begin, grasping for a question—any question. "How do you like working at the Open Kitchen?"

"Love it," he says. "I mean, Jesus—tonight I was the prep cook for a fifth-generation Escoffier chef!"

"Escoffier?"

Jeremy gives me an incredulous look. "The master chef from Le Cordon Bleu? Your dad studied under the men who studied under him, so he's, like, part of Escoffier's genealogy. Trust me, it's a big deal."

"You know his resume better than I do," I murmur.

"Well, I *am* president of the fan club," he jokes.

I roll my eyes.

"What's up with that?" Jeremy asks. "I got the impression that you and your dad are pretty close."

"We are," I agree. "It's just . . ."

"Just what?"

"It's the foodie thing," I say. "As in, I'm not one."

Jeremy takes another swig of beer. "Right, right."

"I mean, I'm totally proud of my father," I continue. "But, like, if you grew up the child of . . . oh, I don't know. Madonna? I doubt Lola walks around every day thinking, 'Oh, my god, my mom's Madonna!' "

Jeremy laughs. It's a nice laugh, deep and fluid and genuine-seeming. The kind of laugh that makes you smile in response, because you feel like earning his laugh is a real accomplishment.

Then, out of nowhere, I blurt out, "Are you working this Thursday?"

He looks puzzled. "I don't know," he says. "Why? What's up?"

"Well," I begin. "I'm planning on going up to Mélange. Late afternoon, probably. Hang with my dad a bit, maybe stay for dinner."

Jeremy's face morphs into that of a ten-year-old being offered a PS3 and a Wii at the same time. "Are you serious?"

"Yeah, totally. My dad likes you."

This last sentence is a bit of a fudge, since I haven't actually asked my father his opinion of Jeremy the Intern Boy. But Mom likes Jeremy, and I like Jeremy, and even

Enrique, who's tough on everybody, really likes Jeremy. So the odds of Dad liking him are fairly strong, though that still doesn't explain why I impulsively lied about it to begin with.

Jeremy beams. After all, I just told him that one of his culinary icons "likes" him. *Oh, god,* I think. *Please let my father like him.*

"I'll talk to Amy," he says. "Because that would totally kick ass."

"Amy?" I feel myself bristle. "Who's Amy? Your girlfriend?"

Jeremy coughs on a swig of beer, and a little spray escapes his lips. "Amy as in *your mother*, Amy. My boss?"

"Oh," I say. "Right."

Jeremy's shoulder nudges up against mine. In a singsong voice he says, "Someone's got a cru-ush."

"Huh?"

"You," he says. "You've got a crush. On me."

"I do?"

"Yes."

"No," I say, though not as firmly as I would've liked. "I have a boyfriend. Max. I told you about Max. My boyfriend, Max?"

Jeremy's grin doesn't falter for even a second. "No. No, you didn't. First I've heard of this boyfriend of yours." He's put the word "boyfriend" into air quotes. "I'm not surprised you didn't mention him, though," he continues. "Seeing as you have this massive crush on me and all."

Now I simply must protest. I conjure up a fake snort and say, "Yeah, you got me. I'm, like, so smitten."

Either my sarcasm doesn't translate, or Jeremy chooses to ignore it, because he says, "Aww. That's so sweet."

Is he being sarcastic, too? I can't tell. His sleepy smile still seems genuine, and his eyes are shining slightly. Is that because of me, or because of the beer? Or maybe he just has really bad allergies or something.

Jeremy leans toward me again, like he did in the car, and whispers into my ear, "Don't worry. Your secret is safe. Your boyfriend won't ever have to find out you've got a little thing for me."

I push him away with my hand—hard enough to make sure he leans back but not so hard that it can't be interpreted as playful.

"You're such a dork," I say, because that's the only thing I can think of.

Jeremy laughs again and drains his beer. Then he says, "You have no idea."

We sit in silence for a few minutes, the swing swaying gently. *Kiss me*, I think. *Kiss me.* Even though as I think it, I kind of hate myself for it.

It's okay, though, because he doesn't. Kiss me, that is.

This is probably for the best, even if it *is* major-league disappointing.

"I've got an idea," Jeremy declares. "Why don't we fight our way to that fire pit over there? I roast a wicked marshmallow."

The thought of Jeremy feeding me a marshmallow gives me gooseflesh. "Sure," I say.

Jeremy leads the way back to the deck and sits on the end of one crowded bench. There's a six-inch space between him and the girl to his left, but Jeremy pats the teakwood and says, "Have a seat."

"I can't fit in there!" I protest. "A two-year-old couldn't fit in there."

"I disagree," Jeremy says. He scoots over so that only half his butt rests on the bench. "Better?"

I'm still trying to work out the laws of physics that will make it possible for my butt to fit onto this bench when Jeremy's arm reaches out and yanks me backward. I practically fall into his lap before nestling between him and the other girl. This is both thrilling and terrifying. Thrilling because . . . well, damn. It just *is*. Terrifying because I just know someone is going to see us and feel obligated to report my behavior to Max.

Max.

I am such a complete and utter toad.

Jeremy's left arm is firmly around my waist, but I get the feeling this is more about him not falling off the bench than anything else. His other arm reaches around me to gather marshmallow-roasting supplies.

"How do you like them?" he asks. "Rare, medium, or well done?"

"Blackened," I say, my voice barely above a whisper.

"Blackened it is."

Jeremy shifts slightly so that our marshmallows reach the fire pit's flame. I can't help myself; I relax against his shoulder—warm, soft, solid—and let out a little sigh.

"I knew it," Jeremy says huskily. "You have a crush on me."

"Maybe," I say, softly, and mostly to myself. "Maybe I do."

*   *   *

The crowd begins to thin sometime after midnight. Those who remain have mostly paired up by this point; even Kat, who's sworn off boys until graduation, has lip-locked herself to Stavros, this underwear-model-hot Greek exchange student who I'm pretty sure has made out with at least half of the female student body at Haley High.

I watch them tongue wrestle from a safe distance. They're prone on a gravity-defying lawn chair, while Jeremy and I are sitting on the side of the pool, our naked feet cheekily nudging each other every now and then. Well, I'm sitting. Jeremy's flat on his back, staring up at the stars.

"Time is it?" I ask him, stifling a yawn.

He thrusts his bare wrist at me. "Do I strike you as the type of person to wear a watch?"

I swat his hand away. "No, but you strike me as the kind of person who wears his cell phone on a belt harness." My hand fumbles around his side until I locate the aforementioned phone and liberate it from its holster. "Crap, it's almost one. We've got to get going."

Jeremy raises both arms and says, "Help me up?"

I'm about to oblige when I realize that offering assistance would require me to stand over Jeremy, thereby granting him a prime vantage point to look up my skirt.

"Nice," I say, with a snort. "You almost got me."

He grins as he scrambles to his feet. "Can't blame a guy for trying."

To speed our departure, I dispatch Jeremy to break up Kat's *bouche-à-bouche* with Stavros while I set off to find Livvy. It doesn't take long; she and Omar are still at the

— 47 —

bar. Scratch that—they're *behind* the bar, sitting lotus style on the rubber floor mat, engaged in a hot, passionate *conversation*. Yes, conversation. They're talking over each other, eyes flashing, hands gesticulating, oblivious to the outside world.

I clear my throat half a dozen times before Omar notices me. "Oh, hey, Stella."

"Stella!" Livvy exclaims, her volume dial set two notches too high. She leaps up and throws her arms around my neck, hugging me with extreme enthusiasm. "Wasn't this the best party? Didn't you have so much fun?"

"Not as much as you," I say wryly, but neither she nor Omar picks up on my sarcasm. "Hate to end your fun, but we've got to go, Liv."

"That's cool," Omar says. He lifts one of Olivia's hands to his lips and kisses it without a hint of irony. "See you tomorrow, then?"

Liv nods, her skin positively glowing. It's sweet, I think. Or at least, it would be, if Livvy's breath didn't reek of syrupy fruit.

Jeremy, Kat, and Stavros bound up the deck. Apparently, Kat has promised Stavros a ride home. He only lives a few blocks away, so he gets dropped off first. Next I shoot over to Kat's, though Liv's is technically closer, because I want her out of the car before she can ask too many questions about me and Jeremy. It's bad enough that he's riding shotgun, his long arm stretched across the back of my seat.

Liv's the next to go; I promise her I'll bring the car back tomorrow, after she's had a chance to sleep it off.

She's too wasted on fruity rum drinks and Omar lust to care. Finally, I head toward Concord Pike, to drop Jeremy off at the Kitchen to pick up his car.

"Save the best for last?" he jokes. I don't respond. Jeremy withdraws his arm from my seat and places it on the console between us.

We drive in silence, without so much as the radio creating background noise. It's loud in my head nonetheless. Finally, just as I make the right into the shopping center, Jeremy says, "Relax, Stella. You didn't do anything wrong."

"I know that," I say, startled.

"You seem tense," he offers by way of an explanation.

"I'm tired."

"Okay," he says. "Tired *and* tense."

Again, I don't respond.

Jeremy gets out of the car, walks over to my side, and leans in the window. "Are we still on for Thursday?"

"Sure," I say. "Why wouldn't we be?"

"Just checking."

As I drive home I replay the evening's events over and over in my head, hearing Jeremy saying, "You didn't do anything wrong."

So why do I feel so damned *guilty*?

Before I go to bed, I send Max a text message saying that since I have Livvy's car, I don't need him to drive me to my interview tomorrow and that I'll call him when it's over. I go to wash my face and brush my teeth; by the time I return, my Sidekick is beeping. Max's response surprises me, and not only because it comes so quickly, but also because of what he says:

Bummer. Was looking forward to seeing you in the a.m. I miss my girl. ☺

The curdle of queasiness, the one that's been forming in my stomach ever since Jeremy felt the need to reassure me that I'd done nothing wrong, intensifies. I write back:

You're sweet. ☺

To which he responds:

So r u. ☺ Good luck tomorrow. Call me when it's over cuz I've got a little somethin for u.

This is great, just great. It means that while Max was taking his younger brother to a ball game and buying me presents, I was off canoodling with my mother's hot new intern and being the worst girlfriend in the history of girlfriends. Okay, maybe not the *worst*. But Jesus. Max deserves better.

Then a tiny voice in my head says, *So be better.*
Impulsively, I fire off one final text:

Thx! Oh & Max . . . I luv you too. ☺

— 5 —

My Sidekick's alarm vibrates me awake at nine a.m. sharp. I don't get out of bed right away, though, because I can still hear Mom bustling about the apartment. This calculated tactic should help me avoid questions about (a) Omar's party, (b) Jeremy accompanying my friends and me to Omar's party, and (c) why I'm purposely getting up at nine a.m., seeing as I didn't get home from Omar's party until just after two in the morning and my lights didn't go out until sometime around four.

It's hard to sneak around when your mother is an insomniac *and* an incredibly light sleeper.

Twenty minutes after my alarm's first buzz, Mom finally takes off for work. I spring into the shower. Timing is crucial here, because my hair takes forever to air-dry, especially when it's so humid out. But blow-drying it would result in a poodle puff of frizzies—not the kind of look you want for a job interview. As I lather up, I practice answering interview questions—"I find journalism stimulating because I love interacting with a diverse group of people"—but my focus is off. Ugly feelings gnaw away at the lining my stomach as I replay the events of the previous evening. Did I really tell Max I loved him in a *text message*? Because I felt guilty about cuddling up to another boy? On top of this, I'm wondering why I *still* haven't told Mom about the interview. What's the big deal? It's not like her affection hinges on me landing a summer job.

I'm too nervous to eat, and way too jittery for coffee, so once I'm out of the shower I decide it might be a good idea to actually flip through the paper before my interview. Of course my interview would fall on the one day a week the lifestyles section is devoted to food. The cover story, written by Patricia Mascitti, a short, perky blonde I know through my parents, is a lengthy piece about a family-run mushroom farm just over the state line in Pennsylvania. I'm not kidding—the whole front page plus a few column inches on the back devoted entirely to the growth and cultivation of local *mushrooms*. These aren't even fancy mushrooms, either. Just . . . you know . . . fungus.

So much for reading the paper.

Choosing my outfit is easy; I ninja Mom's oatmeal-colored linen pants suit and her aubergine silk tee and strap on a pair of nude sandals with kitten heels that Kat left here months ago (I conveniently keep forgetting to return them). Next I tame my partially dried hair into a semisophisticated French twist—an effect I'm sure is marred by the plastic clip I use to secure said twist in place—and slip in the pearl earrings my father bought me for eighth-grade graduation to complete the look. In my brown mock-croc handbag I place a notebook, several pens, and a printout of my resume, which is kind of a joke since all I've really done is work for my parents. Still, our junior-year careers seminar leader taught us that you never go to an interview without an extra copy.

It's just a short drive over to the *Daily Journal*, but one that's long enough to let the humidity spread a thin sheen of sweat across my forehead. As I pull into the parking lot, I say a quick prayer to the makeup gods, begging them to keep my nonwaterproof mascara from melting and turning me into Raccoon Girl. The sprawling gray stone and glass office building looms before me, and my heart begins to thud to the click-clack rhythm my heels make on the pavement. Why am I here again?

You want a car, my inner voice explains calmly, *and you can't have one of those without money, and you can't make any kind of serious money without a real job.*

Right.

Three cleansing breaths later, I push the revolving door that deposits me into the *Daily Journal*'s sterile lobby. The receptionist takes my name and asks me to have a seat in the waiting area, which consists of a long row of skinny blue steel chairs with zero padding. After what feels like a million excruciating minutes but turns out to be fewer than ten, according to the ginormous wall clock hanging over the receptionist's desk, a tall, salt-and-pepper-haired man in faded blue jeans and a celery green chambray button-down approaches. He's got a Hugh Grant–sized smile lighting up his deeply tanned face, and before I can stand he's extending his right hand to me and saying, "You must be Stella!"

"Hi," I say lamely. "I'm Stella."

I wince, realizing I've just repeated what he said.

"Stella, yes," he says. "Mike Hardwick here."

We shake hands, and Mike ushers me up a very long, twisty flight of stairs. "This is the newsroom," he says. "Right this way."

He leads me through a maze of noisy, pale gray cubicles, all the way across the floor to a closet-sized conference room against the back wall. If it didn't have windows, it would totally feel like a prison; it's that small. Mike slides into a tiny, boxy chair upholstered in some kind of tweedy burnt-orange fabric and gestures for me to sit in the one opposite him. This chair's even more uncomfortable than the one in the lobby, and I have the fleeting thought that maybe the office designers picked uncomfortable chairs on purpose so people would always feel the need to get up and move around and be productive.

"Glad you could make it," Mike says, lifting one leg and resting the heel of his sneaker on the Nilla Wafer of a table between us. "We've got something really special in mind for you."

He asks me if I'm familiar with *Snap!*, the paper's free weekly lifestyle publication geared toward eighteen-to-thirty-five-year-olds.

"Yeah," I say. "You guys drop off a stack at the Kitch—at my mom's business every week."

"Of course," Mike says. "The Open Kitchen! That's a great place your mom's got there. Took my wife for our anniversary. Your father was cooking that night and oh—

he did things to shrimp ... Man, it was so good, I would've sold my firstborn for seconds."

I'm not sure which I find more jarring—the baby-selling analogy or the fact that Mike knows all about my family. And since I don't remember any specific etiquette from my junior-year careers seminar that deals with a potential employer who is unexpectedly acquainted with your parents, I sit tight and smile even tighter.

"Anyway," he continues, "the intern position is for *Snap!* The girl we'd hired originally was slated to be a general helper—you know, typing up announcements, checking movie times—all the really glamorous stuff." A bright grin punctuates the sentence. "But once we found out about you ..."

"Found out about me?" I echo weakly.

"Who you are," he says. "Or, rather, who your parents are."

Over the next twenty minutes, Mike Hardwick explains that when he called my journalism teacher, Ms. Duke, looking for a new intern candidate, she gave me a glowing endorsement—and just happened to mention that I am the daughter of André and Amy Madison. So Mike immediately began to retool the job to accommodate what he calls "my expertise." What this means: in addition to having me do the traditional grunt work typical high school interns perform, Mike sees me writing a couple of food feature stories and some restaurant reviews, possibly as part of my own column.

"We're thinking we could call it 'What's Cooking with Stella Madison?' " he says, eyes gleaming. "Catchy, huh?

If all goes well, we'd like you to keep writing the column even after your internship ends.

"So how about it, Stella?" Mike Hardwick finishes. "Think you can help us out?"

I try to beat back the lump that's clogging my throat. Then, slowly, I begin.

"The thing is," I say, my voice cracking over the words, "I don't actually know that much about food."

Mike laughs in these short, staccato bursts that make him sound like a semiautomatic. Then he leans forward in his chair and taps a pen against my right knee. "Ms. Duke said you were modest."

"It's not modesty," I try to explain. "I mean, I've worked for my parents, but just answering phones and waiting tables. And before this year I hadn't even taken a single writing class. Not ever."

Mike nods, like he's honestly chewing over my concerns. "You do know our food editor, Pat Mascitti, right?"

I nod.

"What if I told you that you'd be working closely with her? You could think of her as a safety net of sorts. Would that make a difference?"

"I don't—"

"There's someone I want you to meet," Mike interrupts. "Back in a flash."

In his absence I take some more deep breaths, trying to sort out this absurd proposition. But is it really that absurd? So I'd have to write a few food stories—so what? The restaurant reviews might present a bit of a challenge, seeing as how my idea of seafood comes in a box labeled

— 56 —

"Mrs. Paul's." Plus there's the added trauma of having to tell my parents that I managed to get sucked into their foodie world—seduced by a sweet salary that guaranteed me a used car and insurance by summer's end.

What to do, what to do?

Mike returns with an impossibly tall man who, despite bearing a close resemblance to Dr. Phil, manages to look rather imposing in a pearl gray suit and blue and white bow tie.

"Stella," Mike says, "I'd like you to meet Victor Sterling. He's our managing editor. Victor, this is Stella Madison. She's the new intern for *Snap!*"

I am?

Victor grins widely as he leans in to shake my hand. "Good to have you aboard, Stella," he says. "It's a great honor for us, having a Madison write about food. We can't wait to see what you're made of."

Yeah, well, neither can I.

I spend the next thirty minutes filling out a ton of paperwork for human resources, my head still aflutter. How can I officially be an intern when I don't recall actually saying yes? The point is moot now; I've signed my intern contract for the summer, and legally that probably supersedes any kind of verbal contract (or nonverbal one, as the case may be). But even if Mike hadn't assumed I'd taken the job, I probably would have anyway. The money—the money is like twice what I'd have made working for my parents, and in about half as many hours. Still, I can't shake the anxiety that's making tracks across my stomach.

After I stumble dazedly out of the *Daily Journal*'s offices, still blinded by the flash from the camera that took my picture for my freshly minted employee badge, I drive straight to Livvy's. When I get there, she's sleeping. Not surprising, considering how many drinks she pounded the night before. I debate whether or not I should wake her, but when I peek into her room she's out cold, snoring the soft, raspy snore that precedes a wicked hangover. I go back into the hallway, flip open my Sidekick, and text Max that I'm ready to be picked up. Not two seconds later, my phone rings, and an ultraloud, polyphonic version of "Kung Fu Fighting" reverberates through Liv's entire house.

"Hello?" I answer in a hoarse whisper. "Who is this?"

"It's Max."

"I just texted you!"

"I know," he says. "That's why I'm calling. Hey, why are you whispering?"

"Because Livvy's sleeping!"

Through the closed bedroom door I hear Liv call out, "She's not anymore! You might as well come in."

"How did your interview go?" Max asks.

"Good. I'll tell you all about it when you get here."

When I go back into Liv's room, she's stretching her long, muscular arms and yawning so wide I think her jaw might pop.

"Sorry," I offer sheepishly.

Liv waves me off. Then she gives me the once-over. "Hey, why are you all dressed up?"

I bring her up to speed on the interview and my new intern position. Liv's all smiles.

"Awesome," she says. "Stella Madison, for the win!"

"Thanks," I say. "But enough about me. I want the skinny on you and Mr. Omar."

"Sure thing. Just as soon as you give me the skinny on you and Mr. Jeremy."

As if on cue, my Sidekick bleats out another round of "Kung Fu Fighting." It's Max again, this time asking me to remind him which house on Poplar Lane is Liv's.

"It's in the circle, Poplar Circle. Number eight."

"Be right there, hon. Love you."

I cringe involuntarily and hang up. There's that word again. Of course Max would begin using it more liberally now that he thinks I said it. Which I did, sort of.

"Does texting an 'I love you' to someone count?" I wonder out loud.

"Depends on who's doing the texting," Liv replies. "If it's Max, then yes, I'd say it counts."

"If it's Max what? Giving, or receiving?"

"Receiving?" Livvy's left eyebrow arches suspiciously. "Who's been texting I-love-you's to young Maxwell? Because I know it wasn't you, Stella. It couldn't possibly have been you."

When I don't answer, Liv bolts out of bed and starts jumping around the room. "Holy crap, you did! You did! You caved! In a text message! When? When did this happen?"

"Late last night. Before bed."

The jumping ceases instantly.

"Oh," she says. "*Ohh.*"

This is one of the things I love best about being friends with Olivia. Because without her saying anything other than "Oh," I know she understands that my electronic declaration of love was inspired in large part by my guilt over having spent the night flirting with Jeremy. And when I respond, "Yeah," I am equally confident she knows that what I'm really saying is "Yes, I screwed up, and now I don't know what to do about it." Whereas if this conversation was taking place between me and Kat, there'd be a lot more questioning involved, like "Tell me exactly what made you decide to do this!" Not to mention her admonishments, like "I can't believe you, Stella. Toying with Max's emotions like that! You should know better."

My Sidekick rings a third time, which means Max is out front waiting for me.

"Call me later?" Livvy says, giving me a hug.

"Definitely. Oh, and Liv?"

"Yeah?"

"Let's keep this between you and me for now, okay?"

She nods knowingly, and after another quick hug I fly down the stairs and out to Max's car.

"So how'd it go?" he asks before I've even clicked my seat belt in place.

"Great," I said. "I got it. The job, I mean. I start Monday."

"That's amazing!" Max puts his hand behind my head and draws me to him, giving me a quick but electric kiss on the mouth. "I'm so happy for you, Stel."

We kiss again, this time longer, slower, and sweeter. The way our mouths fit together feels so natural. My hand snakes across the front of his chest, massaging one of his pecs with my palm.

"Naughty Stella," Max says, moving my hand away. "I have to give you your present first."

He reaches into the back, pulling out a small metallic bag—the kind that keeps cold foods cold and hot foods hot—and with a sly smile he tells me to close my eyes, which I do. I smell the "present" almost immediately.

"Ballpark frank!" I exclaim, my eyes flying open. "Oh, Max."

"It's just how you like it," he says, handing it over. "Yellow mustard, raw onions, sweet relish, extra chili, and a dollop of cheese."

"It's perfect," I assure him. I take a healthy bite off one end and offer the dog to Max.

"Naw," he says. "All you."

He is positively beaming at me as I devour my present, and the whole scene is so touching that I almost want to cry. Max is such a good guy—the *best* guy. I can't believe I let a slight attraction to my mother's new intern almost derail me. Kat's wrong; I can't possibly be doomed to ruin this terrific thing we've got going.

So I say it again: "I love you."

"What was that?" Max says. "I don't think I heard you right."

I narrow my eyes playfully and poke him in the stomach. "*Mean.*"

"One more time, please."

"I. Love. You. I love you."

I mean it, too.

At least, I think I do.

The corners of Max's luscious lips are turned upward as he leans in for another kiss, and I let my mouth melt into his, not pausing for even a second to wonder if I have nasty onion breath.

That's how good a kiss it is.

We spend the rest of the day hunkering down at Max's house, making out and watching bits of movies on cable before diving into our next make-out session. Every touch sends shocks straight up my spine, and I can't stop shivering even though I'm far from cold. Max's kisses stray from my mouth to my neck, my shoulder, my arm.

It's not until later, when we are attempting to watch one of the few Nicolas Cage films where things don't blow up, that Max goes, "Stel, I think your phone is beeping."

I pop open the Sidekick to discover that I have fifteen missed calls and twelve new voice messages. I groan, not even bothering to check how many text messages I've received.

"This is going to take a few."

VOICE MESSAGE #1: Mom, 12:04 p.m. "Stella, I need you to come into the Kitchen this afternoon and help get the July mailing ready to go out. Think Max or one of the girls can give you a lift? Enrique is freaking out because I was supposed to buy baby figs and apparently I picked up regular old adult ones. I can't see the difference, but you know how he is about his produce. Anyway, call me as soon as you get this message. It's feeling like one of *those* days."

VOICE MESSAGE #2: Kat, 12:17 p.m. "It is now well after noon and I am still waiting for you to call me and tell me exactly what happened last night. Details, woman! Oh, and that Greek kid—the one we gave a lift home? He's called me *three times* already. I knew I should've fake-numbered him. Call me A-SAP, okay? Bye."

Voice Message #3: Kat, 12:24 p.m. "Make that four times. I'm not answering, of course. Where are you, anyway? And are you getting my texts?"

Voice Message #4: Olivia, 12:42 p.m. "I know you're probably still out with Max, but girl, you need to call Kit-Kat. She keeps leaving me messages to see if I know where you are and if you've returned my car, blah blah blah. Oh, and after you sync up with her, call me. Laters."

Voice Message #5: Kat, 12:57 p.m. "Okay, Stella, I'm starting to get worried. Livvy isn't picking up her phone, either. Did something happen after you dropped me off? Are you guys okay? Or are you both just pissed at me about something? If you get this, give me a call so I can stop worrying. You're really cutting into my sewing time! No pun intended."

Voice Message #6: Mom, 1:09 p.m. "Stel, when you head over can you pick me up a large brick of Manchego? I called Trader Joe's and they have some in, so skip the cheese shop and save your mom a few bucks. See you soon, sweets."

Voice Message #7: Kat, 1:25 p.m. "Okay, Stella, this is getting ridiculous. Where *are* you? Where's Liv? I just called the Kitchen and your mom says she can't get ahold of you, either. She kept yammering on about some cheese—I never know what she's talking about. Anyway, call me already, will you?"

VOICE MESSAGE #8: Olivia, 1:54 p.m. "Kat is out of control. I'm turning off my phone now. Please call someone and let them know you're alive, okay? Oh, and if I miss a call from Omar because of this, I'm going to kick your ass. Love you!"

VOICE MESSAGE #9: Mom, 2:15 p.m. "Stella, where *are* you? Chef Moyer's due in at three and I don't have his cheese, his figs, or the Madeira wine he just now requested. I can't send Enrique three places at once, and Jeremy isn't supposed to come in until four-thirty. Plus I have to get those mailers out. You could have at least called to tell me you were busy."

VOICE MESSAGE #10: T-Mobile, 2:46 p.m. "Your new bill of forty-seven dollars and fifty-three cents is now due. Please pay at your earliest convenience. Thank you."

VOICE MESSAGE #11: Ms. Duke, 3:11 p.m. "Hi, Stella, this is Ms. Duke. I received a lovely e-mail from Mike Hardwick at the *Journal* saying that you are his newest intern! I just wanted to tell you how proud of you I am, and how confident I am that you are going to shine. I hope you don't mind, but your mother gave me your cell phone number. And Stella—I may have accidentally ruined the surprise for her. It sounded like she didn't even know you had an interview! Oh, and she asked me to remind you about the cheese she needs. She sounds rather desperate for it. Okay, Stella. Good luck and please keep in touch during your internship. Goodbye, now."

VOICE MESSAGE #12: Jeremy, 3:33 p.m. "Stella, this is Jeremy. Don't worry about the Manchego; I got here a little early and your mom sent me out to get some. She's, um, kinda pissed at you. You might want to give her a call. Chef's here now, so I don't think she'd yell too much. Enrique wanted me to tell you that in the event of your mother murdering you, he'd like the Pucci scarf your dad gave you for your sixteenth birthday. Talk to you later. Oh, and it looks like I'm clear to go on Thursday, so definitely looking forward to that."

My blood freezes in my veins, and I hear myself blurt out a very loud expletive—one of the bad ones. Max's eyes widen, but the upturned curve of his lips lets me know he thinks it's funny.

"Sorry," I say, snapping the phone shut.

Still smiling, he says, "Seven and a half minutes."

"Huh?"

"It took you seven and a half minutes to check your messages. What's going on, anyway?"

I look at him—his smooth, tanned skin the color of caramel; his slightly imperfect teeth peeking out from his lovely smile; his bright eyes, framed by those long, long lashes, flashing at me mischievously—and I say, "Nothing. Nothing's going on."

I turn the Sidekick off and toss it into a nearby easy chair. Then I take a running jump and tackle Max on the couch. He cries "Oof!" but starts laughing immediately. We tickle-fight for a few minutes before Max pulls me in and plants another near-perfect kiss on my mouth. I know I'll have hell to deal with later—from Mom, from Kat, and even from Livvy—but the truth is, I don't care. I've spent most of the day hiding out in this little love bubble with Max, and it feels too good to let the demands of the outside world make it go *pop*. Who says I always have to be the good girl, anyway?

Max's mom gets home from work around six with his little brother, Cory, in tow. Cory is seven; he was one of those "serendipitous" second children. He's also a little red-headed tornado.

"Stella!" he cries, and then barrels into me with the force of a forty-eight-inch Mack truck.

"Hey, squirt." I ruffle his spiky scarlet hair.

Cory hugs me close and won't let go—he's got a mostly adorable, slightly annoying little-boy crush on me. Max thinks it's hilarious. He's always cracking jokes like "Don't you steal my woman, little bro." Personally, I wish he'd spend a little less time joking and a little more time removing Barnacle Cory from my bruised bod.

"Back up, Cor!" Mrs. Cavanaugh says at last, in a laughing tone. "Let Stella breathe, okay?"

I am invited to stay for dinner. Since Mrs. Cavanaugh's idea of a gourmet meal is the Meat Lover's Supreme from Pizza Hut, I readily agree. Max tells her about my new job, and to celebrate, Mrs. Cavanaugh orders some of those gooey cinnamon dough things as well.

I'm back in my little bubble when the phone rings. Normally the Cavanaughs don't answer during dinner, but tonight, Mrs. C practically chokes on a bite of pizza as she tells Cory to hurry up and grab the handset from the kitchen.

She touches my arm and apologizes. "I hate to be rude, but their father is supposed to call tonight."

Cory starts to shriek in the other room—happy shrieks, but shrieks nonetheless.

"Sounds like that's him," Mrs. Cavanaugh says. "Excuse me, please."

Max's dad is an army doctor. He's been stationed in Germany the entire time we've been dating. The hospital where he works sees a lot of injured soldiers from Iraq and Afghanistan—it's Max's dad's job to get them well enough to make the trip back to the States. Max doesn't talk about his dad much, but I know he misses him. I know, too, that that's part of the reason he tries so hard to be a great big brother to Cory.

"I wonder why he's calling so late," Max says.

"It's not late. It's dinnertime."

"It's, like, almost midnight over there," he explains.

"Oh, right."

We eat quietly at the table while Max waits his turn. Cory bounces out of the kitchen, a big grin lighting up his entire face.

"I just talked to my dad," he informs me, grabbing his third slice of pepperoni. "He's a major."

"Yeah, I know. You must be really proud of him, huh?"

Cory shrugs. "I guess so. Wish he didn't have to be so far away, though."

It's just a simple sentence, but it practically breaks my heart. My dad's foodie trips to Europe aren't exactly comparable to fixing up wounded soldiers, but I know how much it sucks when your father goes away for extended periods of time. I mean, I'm almost eighteen and it *still* sucks knowing that once November rolls around, Dad will be taking off yet again.

Mrs. C comes back from the kitchen and hands the phone over to Max, who takes the handset into the living room.

"Stella," Mrs. C says, "you might want to call your mother. Someone beeped in and I'm pretty sure the caller ID said 'Open Kitchen.' "

I swallow hard. There goes my bubble.

I excuse myself from the table and use my Sidekick to call in. Since I know tonight's demo has already started, I call Mom's cell instead of the main line, and it goes straight to voice mail. A sense of relief washes over me until I hear the beep-beep indicating someone on the other line. Without even checking the number I know it's Mom.

"You're alive," she says in a cool, even tone.

"I'm at Max's," I say. "His mom invited me for dinner."

"Yes, well, thanks for letting me know."

This is odd. I'm prepared for a verbal spanking, not for detached politeness.

"I'm sorry, Mom. I didn't get your messages until right before dinner. But it sounds like everything turned out okay, right?"

There's silence on the other end. Then, in a low, tight voice, Mom says, "We'll talk about this later."

"I said I was sorry!"

"And I," Mom says, "told you we will talk about this later. Be home by ten."

I hang up without saying goodbye, which I'm sure I'll regret later. Right now, though, all I feel is irritated. So what if I took a day off and didn't let anyone know about it first? I got a job today. A good one. And it's not like I was off shoplifting or having wild orgies or whatever. No, I spent the day hanging out with my very cute boyfriend and then eating pizza with his family. Not exactly the stuff that turns most mothers into fire-breathing dragons.

"Everything okay?" Mrs. Cavanaugh asks when I return to the table.

I give my head a noncommittal "yes" bob and reach for the last slice of pepperoni. To Cory, I say, "Wanna split this with me?"

I am *so* climbing back into my bubble now.

I make sure that Max gets me home at ten on the dot. As I climb the stairs to the apartment I've almost—*almost*—convinced myself that things aren't as bad as I fear, that Mom will eventually understand, and that I won't be in all kinds of trouble. Maybe I'll luck out and she'll already be in bed.

But of course I find my mother waiting for me on the leather sectional, reading the paper and sipping a glass of something red.

"Hey, there," she murmurs, in that cool, even tone that's often scarier than yelling. She doesn't even look up from the paper—that's how cool she's playing it. "Busy day, huh?"

"Not really."

"Oh? I was under the impression that you got a summer internship at the *Daily Journal* today. Which is sort of funny, because I don't recall you ever mentioning an interview or anything."

I take a deep breath before joining Mom on the couch.

"I didn't even know about it until yesterday," I explain. "I don't know why I didn't tell you. Probably because I wasn't even sure I wanted the job."

Mom shakes her head. "Now, see, if you'd been upfront about it, and maybe checked in with me once this afternoon, we could be sitting here celebrating. Instead, we have to have a very unpleasant conversation about why I'm angry with you."

"That's just it," I say slowly. "I'm not entirely sure why you *are* angry."

Somehow I've managed to stumble upon the exact wrong thing to say. Mom's hazel eyes blaze hot, and her jaw tightens into a clench.

"Let me be perfectly clear," she says. "I'm angry because you disappeared for an entire day without letting anyone know where you were or what you were doing."

"Max knew," I say. I can't help myself.

Mom folds the paper crisply and smacks it on the coffee table with a sharp *thwap*. I flinch.

"Is that all you have to say for yourself?"

She sounds so much like Bad Sitcom Mom that I almost want to laugh, but thankfully I stop myself before I can piss her off even more.

"Look, I know you probably think I was off having mad, passionate sex with my boyfriend," I say. "But I wasn't. We don't . . . we're not *there*, is what I'm saying."

"Unbelievable." Mom sighs heavily. "Yes, Stella, that's it exactly. I have spent the past fourteen hours imagining you and Max doing it." She rolls her eyes heavenward. "I told you why I'm mad at you."

"Because I didn't bother to run your errands," I mutter.

"I heard that," Mom says. "Once again: it's because you didn't bother to check in with me. I do not consider you my errand girl. I mean, yes, I could've used your help today, but if you'd simply called and told me you'd made other plans, I could've—*would've*—made other arrangements. Has it even occurred to you that I might have been worried? I know, I know—novel concept."

"Sarcasm doesn't become you," I retort, trying to get a chuckle out of her. But Mom merely sighs.

"So tell me about this internship."

Reluctantly I tell her that I'm going to have to write about food, at least some of the time. I find her immediate response—a belly laugh so intense it turns her whole face bright pink—mildly insulting.

"That's priceless," she says. "Oh, man, am I going to enjoy that!"

"You won't be quite so tickled when I'm calling you every five seconds because I have no idea what I'm talking about!"

"You know more than you think you do," she says, ruffling my hair. "You know, I have to admit, it's going to be a strange summer. I honestly *like* having you at the Kitchen. And it's not just because you help out, either."

"I know," I say. "Mom, I really am sorry about today. I think I just needed a day off. Not from the Kitchen, but from myself—if that makes any sense."

She nods thoughtfully. "I understand, Stel. It's not the time off that got you into trouble."

"It's the not calling."

"Right."

She smiles brightly. "Now, if you'll excuse me, I have some e-mail I have to answer."

I change into my pajamas, make a bag of microwave popcorn, and curl up on the couch to watch some TV. Mom pounds away at the laptop, but her typing is so sporadic that if I didn't know any better I'd think she was instant-messaging someone. Bored, I flip through the channels, stopping when I hear the opening credits to *Tootsie*, which is this hilarious eighties movie in which Dustin Hoffman dresses like a chick to score a part in a soap opera.

"Mom!" I call over to her. "*Tootsie*'s on. Want to watch?"

But she's so intent on what she's typing that it's as if she doesn't hear me.

"Mom!" I yell a bit more loudly. "*Tootsie!*"

"What about *Tootsie*?"

"It's on TV right now. Come watch with me! Please?"

I hit pause on the DVR remote and wait for Mom to finish up her computer work. Then I wait another ten minutes while she brews a cup of hot tea and makes another bag of popcorn, which she paints with butter-flavored cooking spray topped with smoked sweet paprika. Eventually, she finds her way to the couch.

"Took you long enough."

"Oh, hush."

We stay up late watching the movie, and when we can't fast-forward through any more commercial breaks, Mom uses the time to ask me more about the internship.

It's almost one by the time the credits roll, and I'm so exhausted I can barely muster the energy to get my butt to bed. My mother, on the other hand, hops back on the computer, which is odd. Even though she's somehow trained herself to only need about four hours of sleep each night, she's more of a morning person and tends to get up between five and six a.m. each day without needing an alarm clock. Sometimes she's out for a run even before the sun's managed to wake up.

"Still working?" I say.

"What? Oh, yeah. E-mail. There's always more, you know?"

"Well," I say, "don't stay up too late."

"Yes, Mom," she jokes. "You should be getting to bed, too. You've got a long day tomorrow."

"Oh, do I?"

"Trust me."

— 6 —

THE OPEN KITCHEN
MENU FOR THURSDAY, JUNE 18
Chef Zhou Yuan of the Five Elements
"A Balance of Flavors"
Cilantro and shrimp dumplings with Szechuan guacamole;
sizzling rice soup topped with Dungeness crab; crispy Peking duck
and homemade scallion pancakes; candied banana fritters and
green tea ice cream

The next morning, I don't wake up until well after nine, and Mom is nowhere to be found. Then I see a note taped to the fridge: "S, your to-do list is on the counter. Have fun at Dad's tonight—please tell him I need the rest of receipts from May!"

I'm disheartened to discover that the to-do list is more of a to-do manual. Mom must've stayed up half the night working on it, because it's typed and itemized by room *and* by task. Hard labor is so not my thing. Still, I need to get cracking if I plan on being ready for Jeremy, who's picking me up around three-thirty.

Jeremy. The minute I remember that I asked him to go with me to Mélange, my stomach falls to my feet. The mostly innocent invitation seems scandalous now—even more so after all the kiss time I clocked with Max yesterday. Still, I can't exactly uninvite Jeremy, especially not after he got so excited when I told him my dad liked him. Why? Why did I do that? And what am I going to tell Max?

"The truth," Kat declares on the phone, after I've filled her in on all the events that have transpired in the last thirty-six hours. "You tell Max the truth."

"You think I should tell Max that I flirted with another guy while he was off buying me a ballpark hot dog?"

"Of course not," she scoffs. "You tell him that you invited your mother's new intern, who happens to worship your father, to dinner."

I point out, "That's only selectively true."

"It's true enough," Kat says. "But if you're so worried, why don't you just ask Max to go with you guys?"

And this is why I am friends with Kat. Because she is absolutely brilliant.

I tell her as much, but she merely grumbles. "I'm still mad at you about yesterday."

"I'm sorry," I say for the umpteenth time. "I should've called you earlier. It was just—"

"Really hectic," she finishes for me. "Yes, I know. So you've said. Doesn't mean I have to forgive you."

"But you will, Kit-Kat," I say. "Especially when I let you dress me for my first day of work. I'm thinking I need something new."

She's quiet for a second, then says, "I'll pick you up in thirty."

"Wait! I didn't mean today!" I quickly fill her in on my chore manual.

"So work until I get there," Kat says. "We'll do a hit-and-run trip and I'll have you back in plenty of time to play Cinderella and still look pretty for Prince Jeremy."

I hesitate, chewing over how much I need to get done before tonight. Still, Kat's nothing if not persuasive, and the idea of diving into the chore manual holds far less appeal than a quickie shopping trip.

"Okay," I say finally. "But it really has to be a hit-and-run."

"Yes, ma'am."

I hop on the computer to check my bank balance so I'll know how much I can play with at the store. Mom left AOL running again, and there is an open e-mail taking up most of the monitor. I'm about to click Send Later, to make sure she doesn't lose what she's already written, when I notice that the e-mail is addressed to someone with the handle "mmmgood." Mmmgood? It sounds like the kind of address you find on porn e-mails offering you "enhanced pleasure" or a size upgrade on your johnson.

Before I even comprehend what I'm doing—spying, that is—I start scanning my mother's half-composed message. It reads:

Managed to get to the library yesterday—checked out that Mark Kurlansky book you recommended—only 20 pgs in but enjoying it—who knew codfish played such an important part in human history? Thanks again for suggesting it.

Oh, and the new intern is working out well, thanks for asking. ☺

Speaking of interns—turns out S will be interning at the *Journal* for the summer—I didn't even know about it—found out she got the job when her teacher called to congratulate her. Felt odd—S usually tells me about big things—we never really had that "I hate you" phase that teen daughters and their moms are supposed to go through—

Anyway, she's been spending most of her time with Max (boyfriend)—good kid, a little bland, but he looks at her like she's a princess and that makes me like him. ☺ Have to wonder, though—what if she's keeping other secrets—or if maybe this is some kind of subconscious retaliation—

See what you have to look forward to with A? ☺

Dinner—tomorrow night? S will be at her dad's—don't expect her back until late—plus we're hosting the chef from the Five Elements and you keep saying how much you're craving Asian—call my cell if

It ends there.

I read it over a few more times, the hairs on the back of my neck prickling whenever I get to the "maybe this is some kind of subconscious retaliation" line. What's that supposed to mean? What would I be retaliating against? And just who exactly is this message for?

I'm clueless on all fronts. What I do know is that she's not writing to my father, who doesn't own a computer and who is referenced in the e-mail. And she can't be writing to Enrique, who uses his laptop exclusively for playing Sims 3 and doesn't even have an Internet connection. For a second I have a paranoid flash that it's Jeremy she's writing to, but then on a reread I see that she talks about the "new intern" so it can't be him either.

I scan the e-mail one more time, realizing I've overlooked the most obvious clue. *It's someone she's inviting to dinner at the Kitchen.* No one on my short list of suspects would need any such invitation. My mom has a few friends she still keeps up with, but most of them she's known forever, and there's not much in the unsent message that suggests that kind of long-term familiarity. If anything, it reads like the kind of e-mails I used to send Max when we first started dating.

And that's when it hits me. The only logical explanation.

Despite the fact that my mother works seven days a week, twelve hours a day, she's somehow managed to meet a *man*.

"You're overreacting," Kat says, after I fill her in on my mother's mysterious e-mail. We're in her Jeep, heading to the Marshall's on Kirkwood Highway, which Kat swears is the best one in the state.

"How?" I demand. "How am I overreacting?"

"First of all, you don't even know for sure that she was writing a guy," Kat says calmly. "But even if she *was*, you can't be certain that there's anything going on between them. I mean, hello? Recommending a book and inquiring about Intern Boy hardly constitute the stuff of a rocking romance."

The words coming from Kat's mouth all *sound* logical enough, but there's a pinging in my gut that says otherwise.

"Besides," Kat continues, making the left onto Kirkwood Highway, "so what if your mom did meet a guy? Would you rather she spent the rest of her life alone?"

"She's not alone," I say. "She's got me."

"Sure, for a year. And then what? You'll be off at college, and Masha will have cast her Jersey voodoo on your father, if she hasn't already. So that leaves Amy with what? Being Enrique's beard?"

"You're missing the point," I say crossly. "It's not so much that she might be dating some guy—it's that she might be dating some guy and purposely not telling me about it."

Kat pulls into the parking lot and eases the Jeep into a narrow space between two enormous SUVs. "Yes, yes, I heard you. 'Subconscious retaliation.' Stella, come on. You're seventeen years old. Your parents are divorced."

"Separated," I correct her.

She rolls her eyes. "Whatever you want to call it—they haven't been together for years. I hope your mom really *is* dating someone. She deserves to be happy, too. And honestly? I wouldn't blame her for trying to hide it. I mean, look how you're reacting, when you don't even know anything for sure."

In the store, Kat tears through the racks, her green eyes like two lasers expertly trained to find the most stylish, high-end pieces for the lowest possible prices. I stay a few paces behind, sulking.

"Did you get ahold of Max?" she asks, furiously flipping through a sheaf of size-eight tops, even though I've told her I feel more comfortable in a ten.

"I don't think Max really wants to hear all about my mother's secret lover."

Kat sighs. "Not about that. About dinner."

"Crap. No." I reach in my purse for my Sidekick and find its pouch empty. With a sinking feeling I realize I left my phone plugged into the charger.

"I'll call from home. We better speed things up, though—I swear, Kat, I can't afford to make my mom mad two days in a row."

"Okay, okay." Kat holds a shimmering pewter tube top up against my chest and I shake my head.

"I'm working at the *Daily Journal*," I say. "Not a cocktail bar."

She waves me off. "Under a tailored suit jacket, this would look stunning, but whatever."

Arms loaded, Kat whisks me into the dressing room. Most of what she's picked out is more her taste than mine, but there's this one top I'm totally in love with—a chocolate brown sleeveless number with an empire waist. The fabric is light and floaty and swirls out from the bustline in pretty layers.

"Can I wear something like this to work?" I wonder aloud.

"Of course," Kat says, like I've just asked the most ridiculous question. "If you pair it with the right piece." She tells me to stay put and heads back onto the floor. She returns not five minutes later with a tan pencil skirt in one hand and a pair of off-white capris in the other.

"See?" she says. "The skirt grounds that top—wear this outfit with those strappy sandals I left at your house that you think I forgot about. And when you want a nice date-night ensemble, you wear the capris. I know they're so three years ago, but the cut is way flattering on you. I'm thinking some fancy beaded flip-flops and chunky turquoise jewelry with that combo."

In the end, I get not only the brown top, pencil skirt, and capri pants, but also a half-dozen other separates Kat's picked out for me, plus a pair of white mules. The total comes to a hundred and eighty-seven dollars, which nearly blows my checking account—thank god I live in the Home of Tax-Free Shopping! As the cashier runs my check card, I turn to Kat and say, "So what are you doing tonight?"

"Not going to Philly with you," she replies tartly.

"Why not? You've never turned down a free meal at Mélange before."

"Because it will be a total disaster."

"How so?"

"You really want me to say it?"

"Yes."

She sighs. "Because if I go, I know I'll end up flirting with Intern Boy. And you'll resent the hell out of me, because as much as you claim to be in love with young Maxwell, the truth is, you've got the hots for Master Jeremy. You wouldn't need to bring anyone along with you if you didn't. But you already know this, don't you?"

And this is why I *don't* love Kat. Because sometimes she knows me better than I know myself.

— 7 —

Kat drives me home at breakneck speed, but when I look at the clock, I am dismayed to see that it's almost one. To get the laundry done on time, I forgo the usual sorting by color and fabric and throw everything into the same load, making sure the water is set to cold so nothing will run. Then I start tackling the items from the manual, working so hard and so fast that, two hours later, I'm breathless and dripping with sweat.

During my five-minute shower I decide to wear the

brown top I got this morning with the off-white capris, because hey, Mélange is a nice restaurant and I'm sure it will make Dad happy to see me a little dolled up. But when I'm out of the shower, applying lotion to my limbs, I realize that Kat referred to this outfit as a date-type ensemble. So I absolutely *cannot* wear the brown shirt and off-white pants. It will send the wrong message to Jeremy, especially since he already thinks I've got a monster crush on him.

In the end, I'm wearing the most demure summer outfit possible: a short-sleeved mock turtleneck in black and a pair of wide-legged black pants with white pinstripes that Kat also picked out for me today. I accessorize with black ballet flats and a small pair of silver hoop earrings. Skipping the full makeup routine, I opt instead for tinted moisturizer, clear mascara, and a quick swipe of raspberry lip gloss, the only source of color on my face. As for my hair, I pull it into one of those casual, messy knots at the base of my neck—a style that takes all of three minutes to achieve.

Yet when Jeremy arrives to pick me up, the first thing he says is "Don't you look hot tonight?"

"You're joking."

"I don't joke about hotness," he replies, in a faux serious tone. "Seriously, you look really nice."

"Uh, thanks."

Jeremy's car is a late-nineties Saturn with manual transmission, and I spend the first fifteen minutes or so of our trek to Philadelphia watching him shift gears with a fluidity that's almost poetic. A Rolling Stones CD plays in the background while Jeremy chatters on about how excited he is to be having dinner at Mélange.

"I mean, of course I've eaten there before," he says, as I continue to stare at his fist. "But never at the chef's table. With, you know, the chef's *daughter*."

I feel a sour pucker form on my face. So *that's* what I am to Jeremy. The progeny of Chef André Madison—his idol's daughter—and nothing more. I know I should feel relieved, but, well . . . what was that whole "you look hot tonight" thing all about, anyway? Was Jeremy merely sucking up to me, hoping to get closer to my dad? Was he sincerely flirting with me? Or does he just go around telling girls they look hot without even realizing the effect that kind of comment has on their psyches and/or self-esteem?

"Why the puss?" Jeremy asks, catching me off guard.

"Huh?"

"The puss. On your face?"

"Oh," I say. "Nothing."

"Don't give me that," he says. "A frown that big? Something's obviously wrong."

I'm not about to tell him the truth, so I play dumb. "I'm not sure what you're talking about," I say with a "casual" shrug.

Ignoring me, Jeremy continues, "It's because I told you that you look hot tonight, isn't it?"

"What?"

"Because you do, you know. Look hot."

"You think I look hot," I say flatly.

Jeremy makes this "sha" sound that I think is supposed

— 85 —

to mean yes. Then he adds, "But I'm totally clear on the boyfriend thing, so no worries, okay?"

The word "boyfriend" lands like a punch to the gut, because in all my rushing around, I completely forgot about calling Max.

"Yes," I say. "Max. My boyfriend, Max."

"Max," Jeremy repeats. "Max, Max, Max. Your mom says he's a good kid. Says he's really crazy about you."

My muscles tense. "You asked my mom about Max?"

"No," he says. "But we work together. She talks about you, you know. She talks about you a lot, actually."

"So what else does she talk about?" I ask.

"What do you mean?"

"Oh, you know," I say breezily, though I'm feeling anything but. "Like my dad, or other . . . men."

"Do I want to get on the Blue Route?" Jeremy says.

Hello, non sequitur! "What? No, no—stay on Ninety-five."

"Right."

Mick Jagger rocks out "Mother's Little Helper" while I try to figure out whether Jeremy changed the subject on purpose. Was he really confused about the directions? I mean, didn't he say he'd eaten at Mélange before? So why wouldn't he know how to get there? Then again, what's the likelihood he knows anything about my mom's secret love life? Because if Jeremy knew, Enrique would know, and the word "secret" isn't in Enrique's vocabulary. If he knew that Mom was dating someone, I would've heard about it five minutes later.

"Want to know what else your mom told me?" Jeremy says after a spell.

I perk up a bit. "What?"

"She said you've solemnly sworn never to date a chef."

This is unexpected. Not only because that was something I said when I was, like, ten, but also because how on earth did *that* come up in casual conversation?

"Well?" Jeremy prods. "Did you actually swear never to date a chef?"

"Um, not exactly. I mean, I think I said something more along the lines of never wanting to *marry* a chef. And I'm pretty sure I said it right before my dad left for one of his extended foodie trips. Did you know he spends, like, a quarter of every year in Europe? Sometimes more."

Jeremy makes a sound that's halfway between a grunt and a "hmm."

"What?" I ask.

"Oh, I don't know. I was just thinking how much that must've sucked for you growing up."

I shrug. "My parents split when I was pretty young, so it really wasn't much different for me than it was for every other child of a broken marriage."

"Not that you're jaded or anything."

"What about your family?" I say, trying to swing the conversation into less loaded territory. "What are they like?"

"Typical. I've got an older sister and a kid brother, so I was totally the Jan Brady."

I giggle. "And your parents?"

"Happily married for twenty-three years."

"Wow."

"Yeah."

There's a long pause, and then Jeremy adds, "I did know, by the way. About your dad and Europe? He was telling me about it the other night. How he never plans where he's going to go, but just sort of wanders around. Although from what he was saying, it sound like he follows the wine more than the food."

I don't really want to go back to talking about my father and his extended European absences, so I say, "Wait until you see the wine cellar at Mélange. And that's just for the restaurant. His personal collection is even more impressive."

This sets Jeremy off on a long monologue about how he admires my father's dedication to offering great wines at affordable prices. He sounds a bit like an infomercial, actually. I zone out almost immediately, like I tend to do whenever foodies go on and on about things like the importance of local produce, the best way to smoke a fish, and the best place to find seven thousand varieties of artisanal cheese. While Jeremy's voice lapses into the *mwah-mwah* of Charlie Brown adult language, my mind goes to Max. How could I have forgotten to call Max? Maybe it's because I'm used to him picking up the phone first. Besides fulfilling his big-brother duties with Cory, playing pickup b-ball games with the guys, and halfheartedly looking for part-time seasonal employment, Max doesn't actually *do* a lot with his days. Truth is, I'm not sure why I haven't heard from him today, unless maybe he OD'd on me during yesterday's extended visit. The thought that maybe Max has grown tired of me sends a little ping through my heart.

"Stella?" Jeremy's voice pulls me back outside my own head.

"Yeah?"

"I was asking about your internship," he says. "I know it starts Monday, but what exactly does it entail?"

"Well," I say, "I'm actually going to be writing about food."

"You're kidding."

"I wish."

"How did that happen?"

So I tell him the story of how Ms. Duke name-dropped my parents, and how Mike Hardwick decided to capitalize on my family name.

"The thing is," I finish, "the job pays really, really well. This means that by the end of the summer, I'll be able to get a decent used car."

"Ahh," he says. "Compromising your principles for the promise of an automobile. I see how it is."

"Yeah, yeah."

"Think you'll study journalism? In college, I mean?"

I shrug. "Haven't given it much thought."

"So what *do* you want to study?" he probes.

My jaw tightens involuntarily. "Like I said: haven't given it much thought. Mind if I turn on the radio?"

Jeremy tells me to go ahead, so I pop out the Stones CD and am pleasantly surprised to find that he's already tuned in to XPN. A new single from Josh Ritter is playing and Jeremy hums along to it.

"You know this song?" I ask.

"Sure," he says. "It's mellower than the stuff from his last album, but it grows on you the more you listen."

Our conversation shifts to the subject of music—favorite bands, favorite songs, favorite albums—and I'm surprised at how much our tastes overlap. Not only that, but Jeremy's seen almost every artist I love in concert at one time or another. He tells me about the time he went to see Cat Power at the 9:30 Club in D.C., and how Chan Marshall had a near–nervous breakdown onstage—how you could hear her playing but how she was slumped so low to the floor you could barely see her. He talks about seeing the Eels at the World Café, and how they did a rendition of "Railroad Man" so powerful that it almost brought him to tears. And he reminisces about seeing them the last time they played Philly before that, and how the crowd was so awful that Lisa Germano ran off the stage bawling and refused to do the rest of the show.

"Wow," I say. "That's awesome." Which sounds lame, but I really am in total awe.

"That's nothing," he says, grinning. "I actually got to hear Jeff Buckley live in Memphis the year before he died."

"Liar!"

"No!" he says. "I'm totally serious."

"But he died forever ago!" I protest. "That would've made you . . . what? Six?"

His grin widens. "Try eight. Anyway, I said I *heard* him. Didn't say I was tall enough to *see* him."

I punch him lightly in the arm. "Jerk."

"Hey! No committing violence against the driver!"

"Well, you deserved it."

"Maybe."

The silence that rests between us is warm, buttery, welcome. Even though Jeremy's got the AC blasting, I can feel the sun's rays through the window. They toast the skin on my arm, my cheek, my temple. I spend so many hours riding shotgun that the right side of my body is about four shades tanner than the rest of me.

"What about spin?" Jeremy asks.

"Huh?"

"The magazine."

"Oh," I say, "*Spin*. What about it?"

"Have you thought about writing for something like that?"

"No, I haven't," I admit. I chew this idea over for a second. "Don't you think it's kind of frivolous, though? Writing for a music mag?"

"How is that frivolous?" Jeremy asks. "I mean, we need food to live, right? But we don't need to eat pan-seared foie gras to live. That's just gravy. Entertainment magazines, they're gravy, too. Good for you in controlled doses, especially when prepared correctly and with total passion."

"Right," I say, feeling the heat rise from my neck into my cheeks. There's a kind of kinetic energy flowing through my veins; everything prickles, but not in a bad way. It's nothing like the fluttery stomach I get sometimes when I'm making out with Max. That's expected, safe. Whereas being with Jeremy feels a bit more dangerous.

We turn onto Beech Street a little after four, making us so early that even the bar at Mélange isn't open yet. While

Jeremy circles around looking for parking, I whip out my Sidekick and dial Dad, but his cell goes straight to voice mail. Then I try the main number at the restaurant, but that goes to voice mail, too. Jeremy parallel parks the car into a tight spot across the street while I dig into the coin purse section of my wallet to find the key to Dad's place. He lives in the apartment above Mélange, but the key to his front door also opens a secret side entrance to the restaurant. I know this because Mom is always complaining about how reckless it is of Dad to not change one of the locks. Still, I've never actually used my key to get in.

A bell on the door jingles as I muscle my way inside. I hear my father shout out, "We're closed!" in his thick French accent. That's followed by a little unintelligible murmuring and then the loud trill of a woman's laugh.

It takes me a few beats to realize that I know that laugh.

I pop around the corner and see the owner of the familiar laugh standing very, very close to my father. He's playing with her fingers and looking down at them with an extremely satisfied grin plastered on his face.

Masha Tobash.

She's the first to register my presence, and as she does, I see her face turn ghostly. She yanks her thin, manicured hand out of my dad's grasp. He looks up, his eyes wide in surprise.

"Stella!" he says. "What are you doing here? How did you get in?"

I try to stay calm as I answer his questions while simultaneously attempting to wrap my head around the image of my father playing with Masha Tobash's fingers. Kat was right—something *is* up between them. This is beyond weird, and not just because it's Masha-née-Marsha, either.

The thing is, I've never seen either of my parents with other people. Not for a single second during their six-year legal separation. And now, on the exact same day that I find a mysterious e-mail my mother was crafting for her secret lover man, I stumble onto this?

"Hello, sir," Jeremy says, extending his hand. Dad shakes it vigorously, both of his meaty paws covering Jeremy's hand entirely.

"Jeremy, how nice to see you," my father says, looking thoroughly distracted. "Why don't you and Stella grab a table in the bar and I'll bring you two a little *amuse bouche* while you wait, eh?"

"Wait for what?" I demand at the same time Jeremy says, "Sounds great!" He starts to walk toward the bar, but I don't move.

"Masha," I say, trying to sound casual. "Twice in one week! You must be completely in love"—I fake-cough to gauge their reaction to my choice of words—"with my dad's food."

Masha's face continues to pale before settling on a chalky shade of bone.

"I'm here on business," she says carefully. "The food's just an added bonus."

"To the bar!" my father repeats, throwing his hands up like we're at a carnival and he's just *so happy* to be here. This time I allow myself to be escorted to a small café table near the back of the bar area, where Dad promises to bring us some fresh-brewed mint iced tea. The minute he disappears I drop my voice a few octaves and ask Jeremy, "What do you know about Masha and my father?"

"Know?" Jeremy echoes. "Nothing. Other than the fact that she's always begging him to be on TV, I mean."

"The other night—at the Kitchen—you didn't see anything . . . fishy?"

"Like . . ."

"Like . . . inappropriate touching? Or kissing? Or whatevering?"

Jeremy laughs. "Even if I had, I sincerely doubt I'd tell you about it."

"Why's that?" I say.

"Because," he says, "that's your dad's private business."

"Not when he's still married to my mother," I shoot back.

Jeremy gives me a long, appraising look. I squirm under his intense gaze.

Finally, Jeremy says, "Can I ask you a question?"

"I don't know. Can you?"

"May I?" he corrects himself.

"Shoot."

I hear his sharp intake of breath, and then a lower whooshing sound as he lets it out superslowly. "You think your parents are getting back together."

I blink a few times, feeling heat creep up the back of my neck. My impulse is to shout, "Do not!" and run off like a third grader accused of believing in Santa Claus. Instead, I keep my voice cool and say, "That's more of a statement than a question, isn't it?"

Dad approaches the bar then with two frosted glasses of iced tea and a small dish of brown and white sugar cubes. "Here we are!" he says, still using that fake "I'm happy!" tone.

"So where's Masha?" I make sure to look him in the eye when I ask this and am not totally surprised when he looks away.

"I am going to sear a couple of fat scallops for you two," he informs us. "They're so sweet, you would think they were candied. Be right back."

The minute he's gone, my head whips around toward Jeremy. "Did you see that? He completely avoided my question! Plus he knows I don't eat scallops because they have the same texture as earlobe."

"Stella," Jeremy says softly. Then nothing else.

I plunk three cubes of white sugar into my tea and give it a hard stir. Little crystals float up to the top like stars trying to form a new constellation. The way my name sounds in Jeremy's mouth echoes all around me.

"I do *not* think they're getting back together," I say at last. "I'm not that stupid."

"You're not stupid at all," he says. He rests one hand on my knee and gives it a little squeeze. "It must be hard, though. Seeing them with other people."

"People? There are people? As in *plural*?"

"Shh," Jeremy says. "Calm down, okay? I don't know anything about plural."

"But you know about my mom, right?" I say. "That she's e-mailing some secret lover man?"

"What? No." He looks genuinely confused.

I take an enormous swig of tea; something catches in

— 95 —

my throat and I start to cough. Jeremy pats my back and asks me if I'm okay as tea splutters out of my nose and mouth.

I am *mortified*.

I'm wiping cough tears out of my eyes when Dad returns with the scallops, but he doesn't notice. He raps his knuckles against the table and heads back to the kitchen before I can even catch my breath.

The front-of-house staff starts to migrate in from the kitchen, where they've been having dinner—Jonas and Tanya, who work the bar; Catalina and Shenae, the hostesses; a string of pretty blondes and brunettes, mostly female, waitstaff whose names I can never keep straight. Jeremy's eyes sparkle as Mélange springs to life; he's got the same expression on his face that my mother gets whenever we go see a production at the Delaware Theatre Company.

Shenae moves us to Dad's reserved table in the main dining area. There's still more than an hour before the first course will be served, and already I'm out of small talk, maybe because we haven't been talking small at all. I've said more to Jeremy about my parents tonight than I have to Kat, Olivia, and Max combined in the past six months.

What I want is to call Kat and tell her that she was right about Masha and my dad. I want to ask her to get in her car and drive up here immediately so she can take over conversational duties and I can sit and sulk and stew inside my head. Let her flirt her heart out—just so long as I don't have to form coherent sentences.

But this is not going to happen, because Jeremy starts plying me with questions: about my internship, about school, about Kat and Olivia—even about Max—but staying as far away from the topic of my parents as possible. It's exhausting, this friendly interrogation, but I'm grateful for it.

The weird thing about the evening, besides Masha's unexpected appearance and instant disappearance, is that my dad is mostly absent. Normally when I drive up for a visit, we'll hang out right up until the time dinner service starts. Then, while I'm eating something my speed (read: nothing Dad would ever offer on the menu), I watch him working the room, talking to customers and charming them with his hearty laugh and Gérard Depardieu accent. Not tonight, though. He's poked his head out of the kitchen and offered a couple of quick waves, but Daniel, the sous chef, has delivered every course. At the chef's table, no less.

"Disappointed?" I ask Jeremy. When he doesn't respond, I clarify, "By the phantom that is my father, I mean. Normally he serves this table himself, and talks about the theory behind each course."

Jeremy shrugs. "The food speaks for itself."

"Yeah, but part of the experience—"

"Stella," Jeremy interrupts. "I'm fine. Really." He smiles and asks if he should get the check.

"Check? There's no check," I say. "You're with the owner's daughter, remember?"

"Sweet," he says. Then he adds, "Boy, you're a cheap date."

"Is that what this is?" I say, sounding flirtier than I meant to. "A date?"

Jeremy leans back in his chair with a lazy smile and says, "It is what it is."

I stare at him, hard.

"How can it be a date?" he says after a bit. "You have a boyfriend, remember?"

But that lazy smile says more than those words ever can, and I feel beyond flustered.

"We should get going."

"What about your dad?" Jeremy asks. "Want to say goodbye?"

"Not particularly."

"Right," he says. "Then let's go."

I ask Jeremy if he'd mind dropping me off at the Kitchen instead of at home, and though he seems surprised, he agrees. The masochistic part of me is hoping we'll get there in time to see "mmmgood" macking on my mother, making this maybe the most perfect day ever. Jeremy, who must sense my dark mood, pops in a Bob Marley CD and hums along with the reggae instead of trying to engage me in more Q&A-based conversation.

By the time we get to the Open Kitchen, the parking lot is mostly empty. No Weight Watchers meeting tonight, or if there was one, it's long over.

"Thanks for inviting me," Jeremy says. "It was fun."

"Fun," I repeat. "Yeah."

I unsnap my seat belt and am halfway out of the car when I feel Jeremy's hand on my arm. I twist around and stare at him, wondering what it is that he's struggling to say.

"Are you going to be okay?" he asks.

"Why wouldn't I be?"

Jeremy cocks his head to one side and says my name in that same soft, breathy tone he used earlier this evening. I pluck his hand from my arm and place it back in his lap.

"I'll see you around."

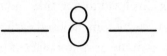

— 8 —

I open the door to the Kitchen, expecting to see my mother. Despite the fact that I'm merely nine days away from my eighteenth birthday, I want nothing more than to crawl into her arms for the kind of hug only moms can give. Instead, I find Enrique taking inventory of the pantry, and Mom is nowhere to be seen. Turns out she's already left for the evening.

"But I can give you a ride," Enrique assures me. "She left me the car."

"If she left you the car, then how did she get home?"

His lips purse tightly.

"Enrique?"

"She caught a ride with a friend," he says slowly.

"A *male* friend?" I press.

Enrique, the Queen of Wilmington Gossip, doesn't say a word.

Not a single one.

"I know about 'mmmgood,' " I say. "But I'm guessing you know more than I do. So spill."

His lips purse even more tightly. Then he says, "Babygirl, we're running low on cumin. Be a sweetheart and start a list for me, will you?"

So I switch tactics.

"If you know about Mom, then I guess you already know about my dad and Masha," I say, baiting the trap.

"Uh, no," Enrique says. "What is it that I am supposed to know about your dad and Masha?"

"Gee, I don't know," I say. "Maybe I should keep quiet. Like how you are about my mother's secret lover man."

Enrique engages me in a staring contest that lasts so long my eyes water.

"Fine," he says at last, letting out an exasperated death sigh. "It's the wine guy. He drove her home. But I swear to god, babygirl, I don't know anything about her having a secret lover man. Seems like they're just friends. Period."

"Mmm-hmm."

"I swear on Miss Sugar's life," he says, gesturing to the sleeping pooch, who's clad in a pink gingham sundress with a tiny straw hat slipped over her ears. "It's all very platonic. In fact," Enrique continues, "I'm still not completely sure that the wine guy isn't gay."

"Right," I say, unconvinced. "Thanks."

"Now dish!" he instructs.

I tell him about accidentally finding Masha in an intimate moment with my dad, and how my dad spent the rest of the night as far away from me as possible.

"That's it?" Enrique screeches. "I told you about the wine guy! And for what? A little giggle action? Girl, I thought you were going to tell me you found them naked. Or at least with someone's tongue down someone else's throat!"

"Don't be vile!" I counter. "What I saw was bad enough—trust me."

Enrique locks up the Kitchen, still muttering about how I don't play fair. He loads Miss Sugar and all of her accoutrements into the car and heads south. A Blue Rocks game has just let out, and we end up hitting a snarl-ball of traffic near the stadium that throws Enrique into a particularly charged bout of road rage. Miss Sugar barks her consternation from the pink padded carrier belted into the backseat.

Despite the traffic, I know I have only a few minutes to decide whether to confront my mom about the wine guy. But even as I pretend to contemplate the decision, I know I've already made up my mind.

It's nearly eleven-thirty by the time I walk through the front door. Mom's curled up on the couch in a pair of pale blue hospital scrubs—her version of summer pajamas—sipping a balloon glass of dark red wine. The mere sight of it makes me lose my nerve, but then Mom says, "So how was your date?" and I blurt out, "How was yours?"

A prickly, painful silence ensues. Then Mom says, "Come sit down." I don't move, torn between wanting to run far, far away and still craving that maternal hug of assurance. I end up splitting the difference, claiming the chair that's as far away from her as possible.

"It's true, then?" I say. "You're dating the wine guy?"

Mom fiddles with the stem of her glass, takes another sip, and sighs. "Enrique. Crap. No, not exactly."

"So what exactly are you doing with the wine guy?" There's an edge to my voice, and the dark look that flits across Mom's face lets me know that she doesn't like it much.

"Careful," she says lightly. "I'm still your mother."

"Sorry."

Mom drains her wine and places the glass on the coffee table. "Vince and I have become . . . friends."

"Vince?"

"Vincent. 'The wine guy'? His name is Vincent."

"What kind of friends?" I press. "Friend with benefits?"

"Stella!" my mother exclaims. "No, it's not like that. We're . . . friend-friends. We've gone out for coffee a few times, and every once in a while, when I'm picking up the wine for the Kitchen, we'll grab lunch at Toscana."

"So you're dating him."

"No," she says. "At least . . ."

"Not yet," I finish for her.

"Right."

We both sigh at almost the exact same second, and Mom says, "Jinx, you owe me a Coke," which is this totally lame thing she says whenever we do anything at the same time. Only, tonight it makes me smile.

Mom refills her glass and tells me a bit about Vincent. He's forty, been divorced for four years, and has a daughter named August, who's almost eleven. Turns out that's how he and Mom bonded initially—Vince had brought a case of wine to the Kitchen with August in tow, and when August started throwing a fit about running errands with her dad, Mom offered Vince some of her patented unsolicited advice. When they discovered

— 103 —

they were both single parents with only daughters, it kind of broke the ice.

"When was this?" I ask.

Mom's eyes cut low, like she's trying to find something buried at the bottom of her wine. "Three months ago," she says sheepishly.

"Mom!"

"I swear, Stella, it's been completely platonic. We hadn't even kissed until—"

"Until when?"

Her cheeks redden. "Tonight."

The word comes out in an almost-whisper, and there's something so sweet about the way she says it that it makes me want to forget this is my mother I'm talking to.

"Stella," she says suddenly. "Are you . . . are you okay with this?"

"I think I am," I say, surprising myself even as I say it. "I didn't think I would be. I mean, all day . . ."

"All day?" she echoes, and I fill her in on finding the e-mail this morning. My face flames hot; it's embarrassing having to admit to her that I'd been semi-snooping.

"Plus," I finish, "what was I supposed to think about you and some guy whose screen name is 'mmmgood'? I mean, really."

Mom giggles, sounding more like Olivia than my mother. "I know. I always feel like I'm answering some porn ad."

"Exactly!"

My mom reaches over and squeezes my hand. Even in the low light I can see that her hazel eyes are shining slightly.

"You're not going to start crying on me, are you?" I ask.

"No," she says, still squeezing. "But thank you for being such a grown-up about this. I've been terrified about telling you."

"Why?"

"Because . . . because I know how much you love your dad. And you haven't really had to deal with either of us being with someone else."

I snort. "Well, I got a twofer tonight."

"What do you mean?" Mom says, frowning slightly.

"I mean that I got to see Dad and Masha in action. At the restaurant? Kat's been convinced there was something going on between them for years. I just . . . I didn't think she was Dad's type."

It takes me a few beats to realize that all the color has drained from my mother's face. This puzzles me at first, until I realize:

She didn't know.

My hand flies up to cover my mouth.

"No, it's okay," Mom says. "It's good. She'll be good for him."

"I'm so sorry! I just thought—"

She shakes her head. "But really—it's okay. I should've guessed."

Mom empties the rest of the wine into her glass, kisses me on the forehead, and excuses herself. She's tired, she says, and wants to go to sleep. "Don't stay up too late," she murmurs.

It's not until she disappears into her bedroom that I realize how freaked out she must be over the idea of Dad dating Masha. Because if she wasn't, she would never have forgotten to ask me how *I* was feeling about it.

The next morning, I wake up to find Mom making huckleberry pancakes. She's got her iPod jacked into the portable speakers we keep in the kitchen and is humming along to Jack Johnson.

"Good morning, my lovely," she says in a decidedly upbeat tone and catching me completely off guard.

"Hey," I say tentatively. "Feeling better?"

"Was I feeling bad?" she asks, like we haven't just had a big, emotional exchange less than twelve hours ago.

"I don't know. I thought you were feeling *something*."

Mom jerks the skillet forward, flipping a flapjack with one expert motion. Then she pops open the oven door, releasing the heavenly scent of bacon.

"You mean the thing with your dad," she says, placing the bacon pan on the unused burners. "I told you, it's fine. I'd much rather find out what's going on between you and Max."

"What do you mean?"

"Well, you haven't informed me of a breakup, yet if I'm not mistaken, you had a date with my intern last night."

I filch a piece of bacon from the pan, burning my fingers in the process. "It was not a date," I tell her. "I was headed up to Mélange, and you know how much Jeremy idolizes Dad. I was being *nice*."

"You were being a flirt," Mom says. "I've seen the way you look at him, Stella. Can't say I blame you—he is a little hottie, isn't he?"

"Mother! Don't say 'hottie.'" I grab two plates from the cupboard and pull a jar of maple syrup from the fridge. "Jeremy and I are friends. *Just* friends."

"Okay, okay. New subject: did you remember to get those receipts from your dad last night?"

"No, I didn't. I'm sorry. We didn't exactly talk much. I mean, I didn't even get a chance to tell him about the internship."

"Well, when you do, please remind him about the receipts."

"Or," I say, "you could always call him yourself."

Mom's left eye twitches slightly. I knew it! This whole chipper act is just that—an act.

Still, I don't exactly take joy in knowing that my mother isn't thrilled about the Dad-and-Masha situation. So I throw her a bone and say, "You know what? I'll take care of it. I know you've got a lot on your plate already."

The twitch stops and a warm smile spreads across Mom's face. "Thank you, sweets. I really appreciate that."

"No problem."

I spend most of the afternoon in my pajamas, vegging out to an *America's Next Top Model* marathon on MTV. At least once every episode I look at the phone, trying to psych myself up to call Dad, but without success.

After six mind-numbing, brain-sucking hours of *ANTM*, the phone rings and I'm happy to see Max's number flashing on caller ID.

"Hey, stranger," I say. "How are you?"

"I feel like death," he responds, thick and slow. "Cory gave me something."

"Can't you give it back?" I quip.

"Ha, ha."

Max coughs then, and a deep, wet hacking sound fills my ear. It's beyond gross, but I manage to croon, "Aww, you poor thing."

When he's finished, he mumbles an apology. Then he says, "I'm really sorry haven't been in touch. But I didn't think you'd want to play audience to my symphony of phlegm."

"Good call," I say, smiling. "Or should I say, good noncall?"

He chuckles, and this turns into another bout of coughing. *Note to self: don't make Max laugh while he's in this condition.*

When Max can speak again, he asks, "How was dinner at your dad's?"

My muscles tense for a second; I've been trying *not* to think about what happened at Mélange.

"It was . . . fine," I say. Then I try to change the subject. "Listen, Max—I hate that you're feeling so icky. Is there anything I can do?"

"Actually, I would kill for some chicken noodle soup."

"That's what moms are for," I joke.

"She's at work," he says. "I don't even have Cory. She took him to my grandparents' house for the day and left me to fend for myself. Besides, I want the real stuff, not the kind that comes from a can."

I pause. I know if I call Enrique, he'd pull some stock from the Kitchen's freezer, throw in a few fresh ingredients, and have me packed off to Max's within the hour. But that would require showering, changing, and socializing, not to mention finding a ride to the Kitchen, to Max's, and eventually back home again. Plus I still haven't gotten the gumption to call Dad, and he'll be tied up with dinner service at Mélange in less than an hour. Although that could work to my advantage: if I wait until I know he's busy, I can do my communication via answering machine and therefore delay direct confrontation for at least another day or two.

Max starts coughing again, even worse this time, and I know what I have to do.

"Sit tight," I tell him. "I'll be there as soon as I can."

I quickly dial the Kitchen. Enrique answers the phone and I put in my soup request. As I expected, he is more than happy to oblige. He is less inclined, however, to offer me transportation.

"Can't go anywhere, babygirl," he says. "Your mom's not back yet, and Jeremy doesn't come in until later."

"Where did Mom go?"

There's a long pause before Enrique says, "She's . . . running errands."

"Picking up wine?" I challenge.

"Maybe. Look, that's the other line. Call one of the girls and get your butt over here, okay?"

Kat answers on the first ring.

"I promise to tell you everything about last night," I say. "But first, I need a ride."

Kat grumbles as I explain about Max being sick, and how I'm on a mission to deliver him some Jewish penicillin.

"But you're not Jewish," she points out.

"Chicken soup," I clarify. "Jewish penicillin?"

"Whatever."

Despite the grumbling, Kat arrives at my place about fifteen minutes later. I'm barely out of the shower and have to answer the door wrapped in towels.

"So what's the news?" Kat asks breezily. "Hook up with Intern Boy?"

"No. But I did catch my dad practically making out with Masha."

Kat's eyes widen into two huge emerald discs. "Shut. *Up.*"

"I'm totally serious. You were right all along."

She tosses her head back and forth, like she's trying to rid her brain of the idea that my dad and Masha could actually be an item.

"There's more," I say, freeing my hair from its chamois wrap. "I was right, too. About my mom having a secret boyfriend? His name is Vincent. He's the wine guy."

Kat's eyes widen even further. "No. Way."

"*Way*," I confirm.

While I quickly change into shorts and a T-shirt, Kat starts rambling on about the parental couplings.

"I know, right?" I say. "I mean, what are the odds I'd find out about both on the same day?"

"Actually," Kat says thoughtfully, "it makes sense. I mean, they're very close—maybe even best friends. If your dad started fooling around with Masha, it wouldn't really matter if he told your mom or not, would it? On some subconscious level she'd already know. And maybe that would be enough to compel her to start something of her own."

I shake my head. "It's a good theory, but Kat—you should've seen her face when I let it slip. She was stunned. Absolutely stunned."

"For what it's worth," she says, "I wish I'd been wrong about Masha."

"Yeah. Me too."

Kat sighs and rises from my bed. "Come on, then. Let's get those chicken meds to Phlegm Boy."

We get the soup and then head to Max's. On the way Kat tells me about how Stavros, the Greek god from Omar's party, won't stop calling her, and how he keeps trying to convince her to go out with him.

"So go," I say. "What's the big deal?"

"The big deal is that I don't want to spend the summer before my senior year acting like a boy-obsessed bubblehead."

There's an edge to her tone. "Finish your sentence," I say. "A boy-obsessed bubblehead *like me*, right?"

"Olivia, too. I haven't heard from her since Omar's party."

"She's busy."

"She's *getting* busy," Kat corrects. "With Omar. And you're always with Max."

"Am not!"

"Are too!"

The sheer middle school–ness of this exchange makes me collapse into giggles, and Kat joins in.

"Give her time," I say, once the giggles have died down. "She's in that honeymoon phase. She's allowed to be obsessed."

"And what about you?" Kat challenges. "Are you still in that honeymoon phase?"

"According to you, I'm in an Intern Boy phase."

Kat sniffs. "You are walking a fine line there, missy."

At Max's house, we say our goodbyes and I thank her for playing chauffeur. "I owe you a tank of gas from my first paycheck, okay?"

"No worries," Kat says. "And listen—try not to stress

too much over the parental couplings. This could turn out to be a really good thing."

My eyes narrow instantly. "Oh, yeah? For whom?"

"For all of you. It's like . . . your parents have been stuck in this marriage that wasn't a marriage anymore. But now they're moving on. And maybe this means you can move on, too."

"Move on from what?" My voice comes out cold, shrill.

"Your mom and dad—they're done. Game over."

"I know that," I snap.

"Really? Do you?"

"Thanks again for the ride," I say. "But next time, keep the psychoanalysis to yourself, okay?"

"Stella—"

I huff off before she can say another word.

This last exchange leaves a nasty taste in my mouth, and I'm no longer in the mood to play doctor to my ailing boyfriend. It doesn't help that Max looks even worse than he sounds, if that's possible. His lovely caramel tan has taken on a green-gray hue, and there are cherry red sore spots around his nose and at the corners of his mouth. He even smells different, like he's been marinating in Vicks VapoRub.

But his smile is just as bright as ever, and seeing it sends a warm fuzz ball straight into my stomach.

"No nurse's uniform?" Max jokes, before launching into the latest round of coughs.

"Sorry. I'll do better next time."

The soup is still hot, so I pour some of it into a big

bowl and set Max up with a tray table on the couch. As he slurps hot broth, I stew over Kat's comments. Normally if Max and I found ourselves in a Cory-and parent-free household, we'd be half undressed and groping each other for hours. But considering my mindset and Max's condition, we settle for sitting on opposite ends of the couch, watching back-to-back episodes of *Ninja Warrior*, this crazy Japanese reality competition series, on cable. It's not long before Max dozes off, though—his real meds are the kind that could knock out a rhino—and I find myself thinking about a bunch of things I wish I could forget: Kat's claim that I'm not over my parents' separation, what's really going on between Dad and Masha, how serious things will get between Mom and Vince the wine guy, whether there's anything real and/or serious going on or about to go on between me and Intern Boy.

And then, this:

Do I even *want* there to be anything real and/or serious going on between me and Intern Boy?

The sad truth is that I just don't know. I've had boyfriends before, but never one I've liked as much as Max. And I've had crushes before, obviously, but never anything as intense as this . . . *whatever* I have for Jeremy. Plus there's the added confusion of liking/kind-of-loving Max and crushing-on/borderline-obsessing-over Jeremy *at the exact same time*.

Maybe Kat's right. Maybe I am just a boy-crazy bubblehead after all.

* * *

My self-indulgent overanalysis lulls me to sleep, and I'm out cold until Max's mom gets home from work and wakes us both up. She thanks me for bringing Max soup but says that for my own health she better get me home now. I'm grateful for the ride, which means I won't have to bother Enrique or deal with Kat for a second time today.

Once Mrs. Cavanaugh gets me into her Honda Pilot, she starts plying me with questions about my new job. Then, out of nowhere, she says, "So things between you and Max are getting really serious, aren't they?"

"Excuse me?"

"You and Max," she repeats. "I see how the two of you are together. To be honest, it reminds me a little how Max's dad and I were when we were in high school. We started dating when we were your age, you know. The end of our junior year. And look at how that turned out!"

I do *not* like the direction of this conversation. The more Mrs. Cavanaugh goes on about her future plans for me and her son, the more claustrophobic I feel. By the time she suggests that I join their extended family in Norfolk for Thanksgiving—which is five months away— my face is covered in a thin sheen of sweat, and my lungs are so constricted that I'm finding it hard to breathe.

Thankfully, we arrive at the apartment not long after.

Mrs. Cavanaugh turns to face me, a huge smile spread across her mouth. The smile quickly slips into a frown, and she places her hand on my forehead.

"Stella, are you feeling okay? You look like—"

"I'm fine," I interrupt. "Just tired. Thanks for the ride!"

I hop out of the SUV before she can ask me what color I'd like the wedding invitations to be.

I spend the rest of the weekend trying to avoid human contact. My need for solitude overwhelms me, it's so intense. Luckily, it's not difficult to achieve, what with Max sick, Olivia glued to Omar's side (in Kat's last text message she referred to them as O-Squared, which made me giggle despite myself), and Mom being the typical workaholic. I set my Sidekick to vibrate, let the answering machine pick up calls that come through the landline, and power down the laptop.

The silence is delicious.

There is one drawback to totally dropping out of life, though, and that is spending too much time in my own head.

Not surprisingly, it ain't too pretty in there.

Sometime between Mrs. Cavanaugh's inquisition and Sunday afternoon, when I find myself staring at the pantry for a full thirty minutes, unable to decide between canned ravioli or boxed mac and cheese, I realize that I've become a rubber ball of sorts. It's like Kat was saying last week—I fly all over the place, never really choosing a direction, just letting myself get bounced along at random. On Monday I start an internship that basically fell into my lap and that became mine without me even bothering to accept the job. I'm dating a boy who I didn't really notice until he asked me out the first time, and now, because he repeatedly declares his love for me, and because he's supercute and supersweet and makes me laugh, I'm embroiled in this increasingly too-serious relationship that is totally starting to suffocate me. Even Jeremy—am I into to him because there's a genuine attraction, or is it because Enrique planted the seeds in my head before I'd met him? Or because Jeremy's such the flirt, and wasted no time in feeding me lines and commenting on my supposed hotness?

How can I make decisions about jobs or boyfriends when I can't even choose what kind of pasta to eat for dinner?

It's depressing, the realization that I exert little to no control over my own destiny. For a crazy hour during *Saturday Night Live*, I briefly consider pulling a Britney and shaving my head as a symbolic gesture of reclaiming myself, but I think I might have a bumpy skull, and besides, it didn't actually work out too well for Miss Brit, did it? Then I think about asking Kat for a head-to-toe makeover—something really severe and different—but there again, Kat would be making all the decisions for me, just like she did when we went shopping at Marshall's the other day.

That's right. I can't even buy a pair of pants without my best friend's instruction/stamp of approval.

And then there's the thing with Dad. I've left him two more voice mails since yesterday and he still hasn't bothered to return any of my calls. Normally Dad's so excited to hear from me that I can't get him off the phone. His avoidance is inconvenient, as now I'm itching to know the truth about him and Masha—if there really *is* a him and Masha, or if she's like the other "lady friends" I know he's had over the years: pretty but transient, and never important enough for me to even meet, let alone develop any kind of relationship with.

On Sunday afternoon, I end up watching this old eighties movie on AMC. It's called *Working Girl* and it stars that blonde who married Antonio Banderas, although it's clear she made the film several cosmetic surgeries ago. In the movie, Mrs. Banderas is this *New Yawk* secretary who wants to make something more of herself, so she listens to elocution tapes to get rid of her accent and reads lots of newspapers and magazines and eventually steals some rich lady's designer clothes. It's not the stealing that gets me, though; it's her drive, her determination. This woman is not a bouncy rubber ball by any definition. She knows what she wants and she's not afraid to get it.

The movie snaps me out of my funk. I get off the couch and into a steaming hot shower. This internship I'm starting—maybe I didn't have to work hard to get it. But that doesn't mean I shouldn't work hard to keep it, and do a kick-ass job, to boot. Ms. Duke wouldn't have recommended me unless she thought I could handle the job, and Mike Hardwick wouldn't have hired me if he hadn't seen something he liked in my clips. So what if I have to write about food? I can decide here and now to be like Mrs. Banderas. Driven. Determined.

In charge of my destiny.

Over the next several hours, I fly into intern prep mode. I iron my clothes, pack notebooks and pens into my work satchel, fire up the laptop, and read a bunch of back issues of *Snap!* online. I push all frivolous, un-productive thoughts (read: those pertaining to boys) out of my mind.

I can do this, I tell myself.

I will do this.

— 10 —

Monday morning, five a.m. I'm up a full hour before my alarm is set to go off. Mom's making eggs when I stumble into the kitchen, and when I say, "Hey," she jumps ten feet high.

"Jeez, Stella—what in the world are you doing up this early?"

"Wanted to make a good impression, I guess."

She gives me an appraising look, then nods, smiling. "I'm proud of you, kiddo. Coffee should be ready in five—why don't you take the first shower today?"

The truth is, I'm not supposed to report to work until nine, but I asked myself, "What Would Mrs. Banderas Do?" Would she stroll in at the exact moment her work-day was set to begin? No, she'd be there early, plugging away before the rest of the sad masses trickled in.

What I forget to take into account is that I am a news-paper intern, not a secretary posing as an executive in mergers and acquisitions. I turn down Mom's offer to drive me to work, since I'm going to be dependent on public transportation most of the time and better get used to it. My bus arrives at the *Journal* just after eight; I soon discover that the only people in the building at that hour are administrative types. The main floor of reporters' cubicles lies empty as a ghost town. Since I haven't yet been assigned a desk, I'm not even sure where to sit. So I decide to pull up a chair and wait for Mike Hardwick in his cubicle.

Big mistake. Not only do I doze off waiting for Mike Hardwick to arrive, but I apparently lapse into such a deep sleep that it takes him a minute or so to wake me up. When he does, I'm completely disoriented.

"Sorry," I mumble thickly. "I got here really early . . . so embarrassed."

"Don't worry about it," he assures me. "Now, let's get you going."

The first thing Mike does is assign me an empty desk. On it sits a sleek black computer and a telephone with a zillion buttons.

"Your orientation starts at ten," he tells me. "They'll go over everything with you—e-mail, voice mail, how to log on to LexisNexis, access the archives, put in a photo request, the whole enchilada. Oh, and there's an intern lunch in one of the conference rooms at noon. Probably pizza or soggy sandwiches, so my apologies in advance."

I nod.

Mike leans back slightly and rests his hands on his soft belly. "So, should we talk assignments?"

I nod again.

"You might want to write this down," Mike says, not unkindly.

"Oh, right," I say. I reach into my satchel and pull out a reporter's notebook and a fresh pen. Mike laughs heartily.

"How cute! You brought your own," he says. "For future reference, you can get all that stuff over there." He points to a major-league filing bank that stretches across the middle of the newsroom. "Top drawer on the left."

"Got it. Top drawer. On the left."

"I figure I'll start you off slowly," Mike begins. "I'd like you to do a profile of the new head chef at Sel de Mer—her name's Sage or Savory or some other spice that begins with an 'S.' Pat Mascitti's got the press release on her desk. She usually comes in around ten, so try to touch base with her after your lunch thing. She'll help get you up to speed."

"When would you like the profile?"

"Let's shoot for Friday. Now, as we talked about before, you'll also be responsible for a weekly restaurant review. Either Pat or I will assign the venue, usually with a week's lead, this week being the exception. You'll make your own reservations and bring at least one dining companion. The paper will cover up to four diners—including you, of course. Pat will get you petty cash ahead of time—she'll explain all that when you talk to her. But you'll need to remember to bring in an itemized receipt the next day. I'd like your reviews by Thursdays—mornings, preferably, but as long as they're in by two p.m. we should be okay—and try to keep the copy under twenty-five inches, okay?"

Another nod. I'm beginning to feel like a bobble-head doll.

"Any questions?"

I fight the urge to nod again, and instead clear my throat and ask which restaurant I need to review by this Thursday.

Mike smacks his forehead in a cartoony way and says, "Doh!" in a lame Homer Simpson impression. "It's a new joint downtown, Italian, called Morte di Fame. Heard of it?"

I have; the guy who runs the place has already booked a couple of nights at the Open Kitchen. But I probably wouldn't have remembered that if Enrique hadn't ranted about the name Morte di Fame, which translates literally into "Dying of Hunger."

"It's more morbid than clever," Enrique muttered. He has a huge pet peeve for restaurants with cutesy names, preferring simple and classic to confusing and kitschy.

I tell Mike that the chef is scheduled at the Open Kitchen, hoping he'll dub it a conflict of interest and therefore keep me from having to do this review. But Mike sees no problem; he frames it as the perfect opportunity to screen "the goods" for my mother.

My other major duty for the week is to start updating the paper's dining guide, which requires fact-checking a zillion details like phone numbers and hours of operation.

Mike excuses himself so that I can "get familiar" with my new digs and the assignments. I have forty-nine minutes until my orientation begins. I fire up my computer, but it doesn't work without a login—a login I won't get until I go through said orientation. Without a working computer, I can't even Google the chef I'm going to be interviewing or look up information about Morte di Fame, let alone get cracking on the dining guide.

It's sincerely hard to look busy when there's absolutely nothing to do.

After another ten minutes or so, I figure out how to

get an outside line on the scary technophone. I immediately dial Kat's number.

"What's your schedule like this week?"

"Why do you ask?"

I tell Kat she's going to be one of the diners to accompany me to Morte di Fame.

"No way," she says.

"What? Why?"

"Because I don't feel like playing third wheel to you and young Maxwell."

"Who says I'm bringing Max?" I shoot back.

"Ah, so you're choosing Intern Boy, then."

I sigh, exasperated. "I'm trying to choose *you*."

She pauses, then says, "Yeah, no. Sorry."

"But I told you I can cover three guests!"

"Right," Kat says. "And that's why you're going to ask O-Squared to go with you and Max. Or you and Intern Boy. Whichever you prefer."

"But if I ask Olivia and Omar," I say, "and Max can't go, then it will be like Jeremy and I are on some unwitting double date."

"So let the fates decide."

It's the wrong thing for her to say—not that she knows it. But before I can tell her about my new, Mrs. Banderas attitude (or formulate any kind of intelligent response at all), Kat tells me that I've interrupted her beaded macramé project and shouldn't I be getting my lazy butt back to work? She hangs up without even saying goodbye.

And here is the major conundrum: even if Max weren't deathly ill, which he still is, he's not the most likely choice for dining companion. I mean, he's no more a foodie than I am, so how am I supposed to pick his palate for material?

But Jeremy . . . I can't have another fake date with Jeremy. Not with my head in this much of a muddle.

So I do the next best thing: I call Enrique.

"What's up, babygirl?"

"I need a favor."

I fill him in on my assignment, making sure to impress upon him how important it is that I have his expertise to help me with the review.

"How did you get stuck reviewing that dump?" he scoffs.

"I don't know," I say, exasperated. "I just did, okay?"

"Not okay," he shoots back. "You know how I feel about that place."

"Then what do you suggest?"

"I don't know. Did you ask Jeremy? Hold on, let me get him for you."

Enrique puts the phone down before I can protest. A minute later, I hear Jeremy say, "Hello?"

"Hey, it's Stella."

He laughs. "Yeah, I know. What's up? How's your job?"

"I've only been in it for, like, twenty minutes, but it's already kind of . . . hard."

Jeremy laughs again. "The best usually are."

"So, yeah," I say. "I kind of need to review this restaurant. . . ."

"No problem," Jeremy says, after I've explained the

whole weekly review thing. "Let me check my schedule with your mom and get back to you. What's your work number?"

"Umm, I—" I stammer, "I don't know. I haven't had orientation yet."

More laughter. Then Jeremy says, "I'll call your cell, then."

Since I can't make the reservation at Morte di Fame until I know which night Jeremy is free, and since I still have thirty-six minutes before intern orientation, I head over to Patricia's desk to look for the press kit about the new head chef at Sel de Mer. Seeing as Pat's desk is freakishly immaculate, it's not hard to find. It turns out the chef's name is Saffron Bell. Not only is she the first female head chef at Sel de Mer, but at twenty-four, she's also the youngest. She got her degree from Johnson & Wales, which even my French-educated father respects, and she spent two years working under this guy Robert Clark at C, which according to the press release is the best seafood restaurant in Vancouver, possibly even in all of North America.

It'd be great to be able to call my father and ask him what he knows about C and Robert Clark and if he's ever heard of Saffron Bell, but I still haven't spoken to him since last Thursday, when I caught him with Masha Tobash. He never even bothered to call and congratulate me on my internship, which is out of character for him. The only time we go this long without talking is when he's in Europe, and even then he tries to call at least once a week.

With Dad MIA, I suppose I could ask Enrique, but he's mostly self-taught and has a bit of a chip on his shoulder about "pedigreed chefs." So any information I got from him would be biased. Mom's usually pretty knowledgeable when it comes to the culinary universe, but ever since she and the wine guy kissed she's acting more like Livvy than my mom. Which leaves me with Jeremy.

It all comes back to Jeremy, I think. Forget about confusing crushes; I need his help in a big, bad way. I can do my background research on Saffron Bell using Google and LexisNexis, but that's all about reading other reporters' words. If I get the inside dirt from someone like my dad or Jeremy, then it gives me an edge. And I need that edge if I want to do a standout job when I interview Saffron Bell later this week. I decide that instead of going home, I'll head straight to the Kitchen after work and see if I can pick Jeremy's brain.

Orientation runs for ninety deadly boring minutes, but at least now I know how to get on my computer. I spend the following hour reading reviews of Italian restaurants and making lists of commonly used adjectives: "fragrant," "well-balanced," "hearty," "savory," "crispy," "crunchy," etc. I also note that each review seems to begin with a description of the restaurant's décor and that reviewers made sure to sample at least two appetizers, three main dishes, and two desserts. Some mention the overall demeanor of the waitstaff, and one even talks about how clean the bathrooms are.

I'm so absorbed in my research that I almost miss the intern lunch. It wouldn't have been much of a loss; the other interns are all older than me and totally uninterested in the token high school kid. Plus Mike was right about the soggy sandwiches. I wolf down a mushy roast beef and provolone, grab two Diet Cokes, and head straight back to my desk.

I am going to ace this thing if it kills me.

— 11 —

THE OPEN KITCHEN
MENU FOR MONDAY, JUNE 22
Chef Esteban Famosa of Caliente!
"Feeling Hot, Hot, Hot"
Plantain nachos with mango-pineapple salsa; classic spicy shrimp ceviche topped with chilled avocado cream; ropa vieja (shredded braised flank steak in a light tomato sauce) served with a cilantro, black bean, and rice salad; guava-stuffed pastelitos and café con leche

I don't leave the office until well after five. This is partly because I've been absorbed in the work and partly because I missed the 5:13 bus due to an impromptu bathroom break. The 5:42 bus squeals up to the stop on time, and as the doors open I expect to be smacked in the face with a blast of cool air. But apparently the bus's air conditioner is broken. As I look for a seat I scan a sea of reddened, sweaty faces and old ladies fanning themselves with the bus schedule. There is a distinct blanket of BO falling over us, and I try to hold my breath as the bus rambles toward my stop.

This only serves to remind me how crucial my new internship is, at least in terms of scoring a car for my senior year. One perk I did find out about at orientation is that if an assignment demands it, I can (with Mike's or Pat's permission) sign out one of the paper's white Ford Escorts with *The Daily Journal* blazoned across both the driver's- and passenger's-side doors. Still, not having my own dependable mode of transportation is going to make scheduling in-person interviews and stuff a real pain in the butt. I wonder if my parents would break down and float me some money against future wages so that I can get the car now instead of August.

Possible, but not likely.

I don't actually get to the Kitchen until six-fifteen, which is bad because dinner starts at six sharp. This means there's little chance of me talking to Jeremy until the post-meal cleanup. Mom's in the middle of introducing Chef Famosa when I walk through the door, but Enrique's on his way out. He motions for me to follow him and Miss Sugar outside.

"So Jeremy asked your mom for tomorrow night off," he says. He is simultaneously balancing a black leather man purse on his right shoulder, grasping Miss Sugar's rhinestone-studded leash with one hand, and trying to light a cigarette with the other. "You look like hell, by the way."

Ignoring him, I ask, "You want me to hold the leash?" But Enrique, taking a deep, deep drag, shakes his head. "And what's this about Jeremy?"

"He got the night off. Told her he's got a hot date he can't pass up."

I frown. "I didn't know he was dating anyone."

Enrique cocks his head to the side, just like Miss Sugar does when she hears a strange noise.

"Clearly he meant *you*," he says with disdain. The cabbie Enrique uses to get to and from work pulls up; Enrique hands me his cigarette and asks me to put it out for him. Before he climbs in, he says, "You be careful, babygirl. It's hard enough to handle one boy's heart. These days, you seem to be juggling two."

Inside the Kitchen, Chef Famosa is readying the first course. I'm not a huge fan of Latin cuisine—the closest I get is Taco Bell—but for the first time in a long time, I'm actually excited about a Kitchen dinner. Well, maybe "excited" is too strong a word. What I'm really looking forward to is paying attention to the demonstration, seeing as it's like free education for my new job.

Unfortunately, my enthusiasm can't mask the flavor of the food. All of tonight's diners are *muy* impressed, oohing and ahhing over every course, but as for me . . . I prefer my nachos 7-Eleven style (i.e., smothered in Cheez Whiz). Plus I don't eat shrimp unless it's fried in coconut batter. Even the flank steak makes me gag. The only thing I find remotely edible is the rice salad, and after helping Jeremy clear everyone's plates, I sneak a second serving.

With Enrique gone for the night, Mom's busier than usual. In addition to serving and bussing tables, it's Mom's job to keep Chef Famosa telling stories, giving cooking tips, and explaining processes and ingredients—kind of like a dinner emcee. Even so, she steals away for a few minutes at a time to ask me how my first day went.

Finally dinner is over, and I quit the game of online Sudoku I've been tinkering with for the past half hour. Chef Famosa presses the flesh with stuffed, happy guests; Mom runs the last credit cards; and I slip behind the center island to help Jeremy finish up the dishes.

"You must be starving," he says to me in a discreet voice. "Did you eat *anything*?"

My stomach—which today has ingested exactly half of a soggy roast beef sandwich, several Diet Cokes, and maybe a cup of rice salad—rumbles in response.

Jeremy laughs. "Guess not."

"You want to feed me?" I blurt out as I dry the dripping saucier he hands me. He gives me an odd look, like he can't translate my question. I don't blame him.

"Tomorrow," I clarify. "Enrique told me you got the night off."

"Yes, ma'am," he says. "Morte di Fame with you. How does six sound?"

"Good!" I say, a bit too enthusiastically. "I mean, yeah. Six is good."

"You need a ride?"

"Sure. Thanks."

"Should I pick you up here, or at home?"

"Home," I say. "I'll want to get changed after work."

"Okay, then."

We don't talk as we finish the dishes. I scrub down the marble island while Jeremy unloads the dishwasher, which we use only for plates, silverware, and glasses, and a hot cloud of steam fills the area. Jeremy glides behind me, touching my shoulder softly as he skirts by. There is fluidity to the way we move around each other, like someone is choreographing this cleanup. We exchange smiles, and the gnawing hunger in my stomach turns into a warm ball of goo.

I look up and see Mom chatting with some regulars outside, and before I can stop myself I say, "Hey, Jeremy?"

"Hey, what?"

"Do you have a girlfriend?"

I can't look at him, so I'm not sure if there's any sort of reaction registering on his face. And his voice is unreadable when he replies, "Why do you ask?"

"I don't know," I say, even though I do. "You know I have a boyfriend."

"What does that have to do with anything?"

I roll my eyes. "I know my mother has told you my entire life story, so don't even act like you don't know every single thing there is to know about me. I'm only asking for a fair exchange of information."

Jeremy laughs. "Amy doesn't spill *all* of your secrets."

"Whatever."

After a pause, Jeremy says, "You have a birthday coming up, right?"

"Yeah. This weekend. We're having a thing at the Kitchen on Saturday—I thought you were going to be there?"

"I am, but that's not my point. My point is, I have a birthday coming up, too," he says.

"Oh, yeah?" I say. "When?"

"October."

"That's not exactly 'coming up,' " I tease.

"Maybe not," he admits. "But I'm going to be twenty-one."

"That doesn't answer my question."

Except it sort of does. When our eyes meet a second later and I see how sober his are, I just *know*. Despite all of the flirting and the coy compliments and the cute "You have a crush on me" jokes, Jeremy isn't actually interested in me at all. And I'm savvy enough to know that when a guy isn't into you, for whatever reason, you need to turn on your heel and walk away.

After quietly slipping my apron off over my head, I do just that.

— 12 —

MORTE DI FAME

SPECIALS FOR TUESDAY, JUNE 23

Antipasto: asparagus flan
Insalata: fire-roasted vegetable panzanella
Primo: gnocchi in brown butter–sage sauce
Secondo: grilled swordfish with citrus pesto
Dolce: blood-orange torte with mascarpone cream

My second day of work flies by, partially because Mike lets me leave early—comp time for dinner that night. I call Kat as soon as I hit the house, hoping to get her take on last night's conversation with Jeremy. Yet Kat is largely unsympathetic when I tell her that my brief nonrelationship with him is "officially" over.

"How can something be 'officially' over if it never 'officially' began?" she asks, sounding irritated. "Anyway, you swore up and down you weren't interested. So stop being such a drama queen."

"I am not," I say with a sniff, "being a drama queen."

"Fine," Kat says. "Then stop whining and go get in the shower. Otherwise your hair will never air-dry in time."

"In time for what? More abject humiliation?"

"Whine, whine, whine!" Kat sighs. "How's Max feeling, by the way? You do remember Max, don't you, Stella? That boyfriend of yours who you love so very much?"

"Shut. Up."

"No," Kat says, a little too sharply. "*You* shut up. I'm getting a little tired of this dance you've been doing. Max, Jeremy; Max, Jeremy. Pick one and give it all you got, but don't string Max along if it's Jeremy you're really into."

"*Now* you stick up for Max?"

"Would you rather I stick up for Jeremy?" she asks. "Okay, then. I've seen the flirting. I've seen the way he looks at you. He's definitely interested. Maybe he's not ready to act on that interest, but so what? That doesn't mean 'never.' It just means 'not right now.'"

"That's great, just great."

Kat lets out a sound that's halfway between a howl and a groan. "I'm hanging up on you now."

Click.

Next I dial Max's number. The reason I couldn't tell Kat how Max is feeling is because Max hasn't told me. He's still pretty sick—at least, that's what I'm assuming, since I haven't gotten so much as a text from him in the past couple of days. My call goes straight to voice mail and I leave another message.

Why are all the men in my life suddenly avoiding me? I haven't said anything to Mom about Dad's failure to communicate, mostly because I don't want her thinking he's all wrapped up in Masha—though that very well may be the case. I also don't want her to know how hurt I am that he hasn't bothered to clear the air with me. The truth is, I haven't felt this disconnected from him since Le Nain went under and almost took him with it.

Frustrated, I flop over so that my face is buried in a pile of bed pillows. I can't think of anything I'd like to do less than head out for dinner at a posh, semipretentious Italian restaurant, surreptitiously take notes, and pretend (a) that I know what I'm talking about and (b) that I didn't make a halfhearted pass at my dining companion the night before, even though I already have a boyfriend (bonus points for the fact that said boyfriend was writhing on his sickbed during the aforementioned halfhearted pass).

The only saving grace is that I won't have to muddle through the meal alone. Late last night I was finally able to get ahold of Olivia and extend the invitation to her and Omar. I couldn't tell if she was more psyched about the free meal or about me saying that Omar could come, too. Doesn't matter—I need the buffer either way.

"I can't believe you put the moves on Intern Boy," Olivia said.

I tried to defend myself, tried to explain that actually all I really did was ask if he had a girlfriend, and that wasn't necessarily the same thing as putting the moves on someone, now, was it? But she wasn't buying any of what I was trying to peddle. Unfortunately, Omar beeped in on our call before I could get the full scoop on what had been going on between the two of them.

The phone rings now, and I lift the handset, hoping that it's Kat calling back to give me one of her famous pep talks. It's not. The caller ID reveals that it's my father on the other line. Now, after almost a week of unreturned calls. I decide not to pick up. Let him wait, like he made me wait.

After a few minutes I call in to voice mail, wondering what Dad has to say for himself. The message is underwhelming: "Stella, this is Papa. We should talk. Please call me."

I put the handset back into its charger, heave a humongous sigh, and head for the shower.

Jeremy picks me up at six on the dot, just like we planned. He is wearing tan chinos, a pistachio green dress shirt, and a dark brown tie with a swirly, leafy pattern in matching colors. His hair is freshly trimmed, and there's a bit of redness in his cheeks, like he spent the day outside.

He looks, in short, breathtaking.

And he smells every bit as good as he looks.

If last night was as weird for Jeremy as it was for me, he's not showing it. In fact, he's his usual jovial self. Mildly flirty, even, as he says, "You're as pretty as a pear."

"Don't you mean peach?"

"Beach?"

"Peach," I say in a louder voice. "It's 'pretty as a peach.'"

"What's as pretty as a peach?"

Jeremy starts laughing, and I realize he's only messing with me.

"Funny," I say, deadpan. "Shall we go to dinner now?"

I'm about to climb into the Saturn when my Sidekick vibrates against my thigh. I'm tempted to ignore it, seeing as it's probably my dad. But it's not.

It's Max.

"I have to take this," I say. Then I step as far away from the car as I can without seeming like I'm doing something shady.

"Hey, you," I say. "How are you feeling?"

"Better, finally," Max says. "I miss you, Stel."

"I miss you, too."

"So how's the new job?"

"About that," I say. "I'm actually getting ready to go on an assignment. Can I call you later?"

"Tomorrow," Max says. "Right now I'm due for another round of meds. Doubt I'll be conscious much longer."

"Okay, then. Get better, okay?"

"Doing my best," he says. "Love you."

"Yeah," I say. "Me too."

When I pocket my Sidekick I see Jeremy looking at me, at bemused expression on his face.

"Let me guess," he says. "That was your boyfriend."

"We should get going."

Jeremy reaches into his pocket and hands me a folded piece of paper. It's a set of MapQuested directions to Morte di Fame.

"I need you to navigate," he tells me.

"Sure."

As we make our way to the restaurant, Jeremy asks me if I've thought about how to order.

"Uh, no," I say. "My psychic powers seem to be on vacation."

"Huh?"

"Menu," I say. "I'll need to see the menu."

"I didn't say 'what.' I said 'how.' "

"I'm confused."

Jeremy chuckles. "Clearly."

I wait for him to continue; when he doesn't, I say, "Care to explain?"

"Well," he begins, "you'll want to make sure to order a few of the specials. To see if they're really special. But mostly, you'll want to concentrate on the basics, peppered with a few unique-sounding dishes."

"Oh," I say. "I hadn't thought about that."

"Don't worry," he tells me. "I'll help you choose. Oh, and we can ask the waitstaff what they recommend. That'll serve two purposes."

"Which are . . . ?"

"To test how much they know about the food, and to see what items the chef wants to move."

"Right."

Jeremy's advice, while much-needed and even more appreciated, smacks me like an unexpected blast of hot steam on my face, and I feel every drop of confidence seep out of my forced-open pores. His questions make me realize just how unprepared I am for tonight. And I tried, I really did. When I asked Pat what I should do, all she said was "Take good notes, and make sure you spell everything correctly." Granted, she's in the middle of her second trimester and has the attention span of a gnat, but still. I can't help fearing that I'm about to screw up in a very big, very public way.

Olivia and Omar are already at the restaurant when we

arrive. They're holding hands, which surprises me for two reasons: one, it's not like Olivia to be into PDA, and two, it's not like Omar-the-Playa to give any tangible sign that he's actually with someone. They're wearing semicoordinating outfits—black on bottom, white on top—but I know this has to be a coincidence because Olivia doesn't "do" precious crap like that. Then I notice that they're also wearing matching pukka-shell necklaces, which are the crunchy granola version of promise rings, and I wonder when in the past six days they've had time to become the same person. O-Squared indeed.

Even though I made reservations for four, and two-thirds of the tables in Morte di Fame are empty, it still takes the hostess almost fifteen minutes to seat us. We have to stand while waiting for her, because the only pretable seating is at the bar, which none of us is old enough to enter. Omar assures me that his fake ID is realistic enough to order us some wine if I want.

Our table, dressed only with dark green cloth napkins and a red hurricane lamp, is made out of rustic-looking wood. It looks kind of pretty, but our chairs, made out of the same material, have small, hard seats and tall, stiff backs and are seriously uncomfortable. Poor Omar, who's almost six-five, has to keep his legs tucked in so they don't touch Jeremy's. Liv goes to take a sip of water only to find a lipstick print on the rim of her glass.

"Gross," she says. "I thought this place was supposed to be fancy."

It's going to be a long night.

I resist the urge to apologize to everyone, and bury my

head in the extralarge menu. With Jeremy's advice echoing in my ears, I start choosing what I'll order. But then I second-guess myself almost immediately. I slip my reporter's notebook out of my purse and start scratching a list of what I think I should get on it, and then pass it over to Jeremy. He gives me a funny look, but instead of teasing me like I half expect him to, he makes some notes on my list and hands it back to me. "Nix the flan—get the bruschetta three ways," he's written. He's placed checkmarks next to the panzanella, the gnocchi, and my choice of dessert (the orange torte).

Olivia and Omar are dissecting the menu together, whispering. Jeremy pulls my reporter's notebook back toward him, writes some stuff down, and passes the notebook to O-Squared. Omar nods at Jeremy, a gesture I take to mean "Got it," but I'm feeling too chicken to ask either of them what's going on.

As if he can read my mind, Jeremy leans toward me and says in a low voice, "I told them what we're ordering, and then asked them to get different things, so we can sample more of the menu."

"Right," I say. *Duh.* "Thanks."

"That's what I'm here for."

He smiles at me, a warm, comforting smile. Then he reaches over and gives my hand a reassuring squeeze. It's not a romantic gesture—not by any stretch—but the touch of his skin against mine sends sparks up my spine.

Our waiter comes and introduces himself. His name is Colin and he is immaculate in his appearance; it looks like even his apron has been starched and ironed. He asks if we'd like to see a wine list, and Omar's about to say yes when Jeremy cuts in and tells Colin that we're all underage.

"Whoops!" Colin says, covering his mouth and giggling. He puts his order pad back into his apron pocket and starts to walk away.

Liv calls out, "Um, excuse me? Colin?" and when Colin doesn't stop, Omar bellows, "Yo, dude—we've got a situation with a dirty glass!" Colin scurries back over and apologizes. He tries to sound sincere, but I can see how tight his face looks as he takes the offending glass from Liv.

Jeremy says, "I don't know about the rest of you guys, but I'd love an iced tea."

"Diet Coke," I say, and Olivia says her, too, and can she please get a fresh glass of water? Omar, after much deliberation, settles for water only.

"Service is impressive," Jeremy notes wryly.

Unfortunately, the service doesn't improve over the span of the meal. Colin doesn't take our appetizer order when he brings the drinks, saying he'll be right back, but ten minutes later he still hasn't reappeared. So Jeremy gets up and quietly lets the hostess know that we're looking for our waiter.

When Colin returns to the table, he doesn't look happy. At least this time he takes our orders—not just for the apps but also for our entrees.

Two hours later, the meal comes to a close. I have seventeen pages of notes and absolutely no idea what I'm going to write or how to write it. I tried hard to concentrate on the food and the flavors, but the bad service and O-Squared's growing irritation were definite detractors. Plus I spent most of the meal trying to read Jeremy's reaction to every bite he took, though he gave away nothing. Even on the ride home, he refuses to tell me what he thinks.

"Go write your review," he says. "Then I'll tell you my opinion."

I make him promise to read it over tomorrow night.

"Of course," he says, slowing the car down and putting on the turn signal.

"Where are we going?"

But he doesn't have to answer, because the next thing I know, we're pulling into a Burger King drive-thru.

"My hero!" I say, practically swooning.

We order two Double Whoppers with cheese and eat them in the parking lot.

"Does this mean you hated the food?" I ask, between greedy mouthfuls of grease and cheese.

"Nice try," he says. Then he reaches forward and brushes his thumb against the corner of my mouth. "You're bleeding ketchup." He brings his thumb to his own mouth and sucks off the red goo. I momentarily lose the ability to breathe.

"I should get you home," Jeremy says. He polishes off the last of his burger and puts the car in gear.

The bouncy-rubber-ball feeling returns as I stare absentmindedly out the car window. What am I doing? What do I *want* to be doing? Actually, that's an easy one: what I want to be doing is kissing Jeremy. I'm more certain of that than anything else. The place where his thumb touched my mouth throbs hungrily. It's demanding kisses, even more than my heart.

Jeremy pulls up to the town house and puts the car in park. Spasms erupt in my chest, and a silent devil voice whispers in my ear, "Go on, do it. Kiss him. You know you want to. Kiss him now."

Slowly I turn my head, trying to muster up the courage to follow the devil voice. I might have done it, too, if there weren't suddenly headlights flooding the interior of the car.

"Your mom?" Jeremy guesses.

I look at the clock on the dash and see it's just past nine. "No, it's too early."

"Must be a neighbor, then."

"Yeah."

The moment is lost. There will be no kissing tonight, that's for sure.

Before I get out, I make Jeremy promise again that he'll read my review tomorrow tonight.

"It has to be tomorrow," I say for the third time.

"I know," Jeremy says. "It's due Thursday. Go get some rest, okay?"

I start to walk away and then stop and walk back toward Jeremy's car. He rolls down the window, and I lean in.

"In case you were wondering," I say, "this was the best nondate I've been on in, like, forever."

I worry that I've overstepped my bounds, but Jeremy gives me another one of those warm, comforting smiles.

"Ditto," he says. Then I watch him drive away.

When I turn toward the house, I see who pulled up behind us: Olivia. She's standing outside the front door, sans Omar, her jaw dropped halfway to the ground.

"Kit-Kat was right," she says. "You *are* making a play for Intern Boy."

"No," I shoot back, even though it's kinda sorta true.

"Don't you lie to me, girl. Even Omar could see the lightning crackling between the two of you."

"Really?"

"Really," she says flatly. "Let me in. We need to talk."

Inside, Livvy helps herself to a glass of lavender lemonade (my mother's summer specialty) while I flit between the kitchen and living rooms, tidying up piles that don't exactly need to be tidied.

"Things between you and Omar seem good," I say, trying to sound nonchalant. It doesn't work.

"They are, but don't change the subject. What's going on with you? What are you doing, Stella?"

"I don't know!" I say loudly, slamming a stack of magazines down for emphasis. Olivia winces at the sound. "Sorry," I mumble.

After a pause, Liv says, "No one's judging here, Stel."

"Sure they are," I say. "I mean, *I* am. I am judging me."

Livvy's eyes soften, and I have to look away or else I'll start crying.

"It's like I have no control," I say miserably. "Whenever I'm with him, I just . . . I just want to touch him. Or kiss him. Or whatever. But then I think about Max . . . and when I'm with Max, I want to be his girlfriend. The *best* girlfriend. I can't wrap my mind around any of it."

"Who says has you have to?" Olivia asks.

"What do you mean?"

"I mean, what exactly is it that you have to wrap your mind around? The fact that you're seventeen and you have a hot high school boyfriend and an even hotter older guy flirting with you constantly? The fact that you're attracted to both? The fact that you're a red-blooded teenager getting off on the reality of two eligible bachelors vying for your attention and affection?

"This is normal, Stella," Liv continues. "You're a young, foxy babe. Guys are going to want you, and no, they're not always going to wait their turn. The only thing you really have to wrap your mind around is how you're going to tell young Maxwell that he's not the only guy occupying your heart."

I gasp. "But how can I do that? He'll be so completely *hurt*."

"He'll be more hurt if he finds out you've hooked up with another guy while you're supposedly still his girlfriend," Liv points out. "Let me ask you this—do you want to hook up with Jeremy? Honestly, if the opportunity presented itself, would you?"

I think about that moment right before Liv pulled up behind us, and how determined I was to try to ninja a kiss.

I nod.

"Then there's your answer!" Livvy says. "You have to talk to Max. Tell him you're into someone else. You don't have to break up with him, not if you don't want to."

"Don't you think he's going to want to dump me? I mean, here I am, throwing around the L-word and not a week later telling him I have the hots for someone other than him?"

"Someone in *addition* to him," Liv corrects. "There is a difference. And yes, maybe he will be so hurt that he'll end things right there. Or maybe he'll understand that the two of you are virtual babies in terms of social development, and slow things down a bit. I mean, Stel—I do like Max and all, but there's something about him that makes me think he's gunning for marriage."

"His parents were high school sweethearts," I explain. "They got married at eighteen, right before his dad went to boot camp."

Livvy nods thoughtfully. "That'd do it. I saw this shrink on Tyra Banks's show and he was talking about how we try to emulate whatever models of love we've grown up around. Like how girls who watched their moms get beaten end up with abusive boyfriends. That's probably why you, unlike Max, are so indecisive and noncommittal."

I feel my eyes narrow slightly, and a deep frown tugs down on the corners of my mouth. "What are you talking about?"

She takes a second, like she's choosing her words carefully. "I just mean . . . well, like how your parents have been separated for so long but not actually divorced. That has to have been confusing for you. Wondering if the split was real, if they were ever getting back together . . ."

"Stop," I say sharply. "You don't know what you're talking about, so just stop."

"Okay," she says. "Sorry."

Livvy gives me a hug and tells me to call her if I need anything, no matter what the time.

"It's going to be okay," she says.

"I hope so," I say. "I really do."

— 13 —

THE OPEN KITCHEN
MENU FOR WEDNESDAY, JUNE 24
Chef Ava Mandylor of the Fig Tree
"Food Fit for the Gods"
Four-olive hummus with toasted pita chips; fried-goat-cheese-and-
fig salad in a Greek yogurt dressing; marinated lamb souvlaki with
melted feta, grilled lemon-dill artichoke hearts, and zucchini fries;
walnut cream–filled phyllo puffs dusted with fresh-ground nutmeg

Tonight's bus is the third one this week that has absolutely no air conditioning, and as I sweat in my seat I fight the urge to cry. My Sidekick vibrates in my bag, and I go to answer it, but when I see it's Max calling—I totally forgot that I was supposed to give him a ring today—I let it go to voice mail. I can't deal with him. Not yet, anyway.

I spent my entire eight-hour workday trolling through my notes from dinner and trying to write a review that sounds vaguely intelligent or, at the very least, somewhat informed. This is a task easier said than done. I pounded the keys all morning long, and by noon, all I had was:

Morte di Fame is the hot new Italian eatery in downtown Wilmington. It's warm, inviting atmosphere, helpful waitstaff, and inventive take on a classic menu left this restaurant-goer wanting more, more, more.

It took me a dozen rereads to realize I mistakenly placed an apostrophe in "its." Sadly, this wasn't my biggest problem. Besides the part about me leaving wanting more (I was *starving*), it's mostly poorly written BS.

When I arrive at the Kitchen, Jeremy takes one look at me and knows. I know he knows because his eyes get really big and soft, and there's the faintest hint of a sympathetic smile playing on the corners of his lips. He winks his acknowledgment before getting back to chopping up some artichokes.

I sink into a chair near the computer. Mom's on the phone, holding up her "give me a sec" finger. As I sit there, I marvel over the whole concept of body language and how people can have entire conversations without ever saying a word.

She hangs up. "Hey, sweets. I didn't know you were coming in tonight."

"I didn't either," I say. "But I'm kind of floundering on this restaurant review, and Jeremy promised to help me, so . . ."

"Jeremy," she repeats.

"Don't start that again," I say. "He's my friend, and he's helping me. That's all."

"Sure."

"Hey, where's Enrique? Did he go home early again?"

She shakes her head. "He's at the vet. Miss Sugar's been throwing up all day. He thinks she got into the onion crock, because he found a flake of purple skin in the pantry. Normally I'd think he was being his usual drama-queen self, but I've never seen that dog shake so hard. She really is sick on something. Give him a call—I'm sure he'd be happy to hear from you."

I grab the phone and quickly dial Enrique's cell. He answers with a peevish "What?"

"It's me," I say. "I just heard. How's the princess doing?"

Enrique sighs, hard. "It's not good. She lost a full pound and a half, so they've got her strapped to an IV. Dr. Lindsay wants to run some tests, but she can't until she's better hydrated."

"Was it really the onions?"

"I don't think so," he says. "They don't know what it is."

I hear the anguish in his voice and make a snap decision. "I'll be right there."

The dining room is starting to fill with guests, and Chef Ava is quietly issuing orders to Jeremy. I have my pathetic attempt at an article folded in my pocket. It can wait. When I get Jeremy's attention, I ask him if I can borrow his car. "Enrique took Mom's to the vet and he's really kind of a mess."

"Can you drive stick?"

"Of course."

Jeremy nods, disappears into the back, and returns with his keys. "She might need some gas."

"I'll fill it up, I promise."

As I turn to walk away, I hear Jeremy ask, "Are we still on for tonight?"

"Yeah," I say. "Desperately."

We exchange grins. I tell Mom I'm taking Jeremy's car to the vet's office to give Enrique some moral support. She slips me a twenty for gas, gives me a quick hug, and sends me on my way.

Enrique's vet operates out of a large chain pet store in a strip mall on the other end of Concord Pike. When I get there, it looks like the office part is closing down. Enrique is crouched on a wooden bench outside the grooming salon that also operates out of the store. Upon seeing me, he springs up and runs to give me a clutchlike hug.

"Thank you, babygirl," he whispers. When he pulls away, I see that his eyes are pink from crying.

I know I make fun of Miss Sugar and the way Enrique treats her like she's his furry, fashionista child, but the truth is, his love for that dog runs deeper than anything I've seen or felt in years. It makes me wonder if a pet is in any way capable of understanding how lucky it is to be adopted by someone so devoted. We sit on a nearby bench, waiting for the doctor to emerge. I rub his back and tell him that everything's going to be okay.

After another twenty minutes or so, the vet emerges. "She's going to be fine," she declares, and Enrique starts to shake even more.

"So what's wrong with her?" I ask.

"Honestly? We don't know for sure," she says. "But dogs are like that. When they don't feel good, they'll eat grass or whatever to make themselves throw up. But there aren't any signs of poison or anything more serious than an upset tummy."

She tells us she's weaning Miss Sugar off the IV and

that Enrique will have to watch her level of hydration for a few days. She prescribes some low-residue dog food and suggests that Enrique feed the pooch a syringeful of Pedialyte twice a day until her weight returns to normal.

A nurse brings Miss Sugar out on her pink flowered leash, and Enrique drops to his knees to embrace her. She licks kisses all over his face, and he coos private things to her in that baby voice crazy dog people use to speak to their pets. Instead of rolling my eyes, however, I feel them get a little misty.

Enrique assures me he's okay to drive, and we both head back to the Kitchen, him in Mom's car, me in Jeremy's. I swing into the Burger King drive-thru on my way back, as tonight's chef is serving lamb and no way am I eating the subject of countless nursery rhymes. It just seems . . . perverse.

Back at the Kitchen, Mom asks me to give Enrique a ride home, which I do. When I get back, the diners are polishing off their desserts. Jeremy's already doing a load of dishes by hand. I slip behind the island, pull on an apron, and start drying.

An hour later, the place is empty, spotless, and ours. Mom was in a rush to get out of the Kitchen; she and Vince must've had plans or a phone date or something, because she didn't blink an eye when I told her I'd lock up and Jeremy would drop me off later. In fact, she was yelling goodnight when she was already halfway out the door.

Jeremy reads over my draft a few times. Then he looks

up and says, "Does Gordon have you on the payroll or something?"

"Gordon?" I repeat, clueless.

"Gordon Jenkins," he says. "The head chef? Who you should probably mention somewhere in here."

I feel myself blush.

"Did you really think the atmosphere was 'warm and inviting'?" Jeremy asks.

I shrug.

"Why are you calling the waitstaff 'helpful'? They were a bunch of bumbling idiots. It took half an hour to get Liv a clean glass of water!"

"Maybe that was just our waiter," I offer.

Jeremy shakes his head. "The hostess was terrible, too. There was no excuse, either. The house was practically empty. Speaking of," he continues, "what gave you the impression that this was a 'hot new eatery'? We were, like, half the night's patronage."

"Fine!" I say huffily. "I suck, okay? I never wanted this stupid job to begin with!"

"Whoa," Jeremy says. "Calm down, there. I didn't say you suck. I was just wondering why you wrote some of the things you did."

"Things that suck," I say, sniffling.

"Okay, yeah," he says after a pause. "It pretty much sucks. But that doesn't mean *you* suck. Stella, I've talked to you enough to know your voice. And this isn't your voice. This is you trying to play restaurant critic instead of being one. It sounds generic and inauthentic. You can do better than this. I'm absolutely certain of that."

I tell him that my sucktastic review took me an entire day to write. In response, he picks up the paper and rips it into a bunch of chunky pieces.

"Time to start over," he declares.

While I sit stunned, Jeremy starts running back and forth to the pantry, gathering ingredients.

"What are you doing?" I ask.

"*We*," he says, "are going to cook."

I'm instantly alarmed. "Cook what?"

"Gnocchi in a brown butter–sage sauce."

"And why is this?"

Jeremy grabs a saucepan and fills it with water. "To teach you how to write about food."

"Learning by doing," I say.

"Learning by *tasting*," he corrects.

There aren't many ingredients in the gnocchi, just a large potato, one egg, and some flour. Jeremy gently drops the potato into his pot of boiling water, explaining that he's left it whole in its jacket to keep out as much moisture as possible. "Gnocchi," he says, "is best when it's made from a high-starch, low-moisture potato. The more moisture in the potato, the gummier the dumplings get."

"So the gnocchi we had last night—that was made from a potato superhigh in moisture, right?"

Jeremy laughs. "Actually, I'm almost a hundred percent certain they weren't fresh. They had the chemical taste of preprepared gnocchi—pretty much unacceptable in my book."

Next, Jeremy grabs a bunch of fresh sage, which looks a little like pale green velvet leaves on a stem. "We're going to do a chiffonade," he explains. "Do you know what that is?"

"Ribbons," I say.

Jeremy looks startled.

"Just because I don't like being around foodies doesn't mean I haven't picked up a few things along the way. Did you forget who my father is?"

"Touché."

Jeremy decides that I'm going to do the honors. He shows me how to gather the soft leaves and bundle them into a tight coil, then run the knife through the bunch in tiny increments, turning the sage into a pile of thin, ribbonlike slivers.

While the potato continues to boil, Jeremy gives me an egg and a small bowl in which to crack and beat it. Then he hands me a large skillet and tells me to turn the stove to medium heat. Next I put a stick of butter into the pan and push it around with a wooden spoon, waiting for it to melt and start to brown.

Jeremy takes a tasting spoon from the crock on the island, dips the back of it into a bit of melted butter and tells me to taste.

"Yeah," I say, "it's butter."

He takes a second spoon and dips it into the butter, too. "This time, I want you to *taste* it."

I'm not sure what he's getting at, but I do it anyway.

In a couple of minutes, the butter has turned foamy and caramel-colored. Jeremy tells me to turn off the heat, runs a third tasting spoon through the pan, and tells me to taste again.

— 157 —

"It's different," I say, surprised. "It tastes . . . I don't know. Nutty or something."

Jeremy smiles. "Excellent."

He scoops up my sage ribbons and transfers them to the skillet. Some of the pieces frizzle in the hot butter. It smells like a wet fall morning. I say this to Jeremy, and his smile grows bigger.

"Good. Smells are good." He picks up one of the sage leaves I haven't cut and has me smell it.

"Like trees," I say. "Or like sweet dirt, the kind that's just been fertilized."

He nods. "The culinary way of saying that is 'earthy.' But yeah—bang on."

Another tasting spoon is whipped out of the crock and put back into the butter mixture. Again I'm told to taste.

There's a distinct difference between the melted butter, the browned butter, and the browned butter infused with sage. Now the mixture isn't just nutty, it's *earthy*.

"I get it," I say. "Earthy. Yes. Wow."

We return our attention to the potato, which is out of the water and cooling a bit. Jeremy cuts the potato and hands me a half, instructing me to scoop the mealy flesh out of the skin. It's still too hot to touch, so we hold the potato halves in tea towels while we scoop. Once that's done, I'm given a fork and told to mash up the meal in the bowl. Jeremy gives it a generous pinch of kosher salt and a few turns of the pepper grinder, then carefully adds a few tablespoons of my beaten egg. I mash on.

Finally we sift some flour over the mixture. Then Jeremy plunges his hands into the bowl and starts to knead all the ingredients into a dough.

— 158 —

"Wait," I say. "Let me do it."

"Not too much," he tells me. "Just enough to blend it all together. If you overwork it, you'll produce too much gluten, which is another thing that makes the gnocchi taste gummy."

Jeremy sections the dough into four pieces and hands me one. We stand next to each other over the marble island, rolling our dough into a long rope. I feel like our bodies are working in the same rhythm again, and the mere thought gives me gooseflesh.

Next we cut our ropes into inch-long pieces, which are then rolled over the tines of a fork. I ask Jeremy if this is purely decorative.

"Good question," he says approvingly. "The little grooves are cute, but really, they help trap the sauce over the dumpling."

"Nice."

When all the dough has been made into small ridged gnocchi, Jeremy has me gently lower them into a shallow pan of salted water. The gnocchi slowly float to the top, and in four minutes, I'm using a slotted spoon to transfer them from the water into two bowls. Jeremy uses a small ladle to pour a bit of the browned butter sauce over our dumplings. Then he takes a hunk of fresh Parmesan and grates a generous mound over the tops of our bowls.

I stab my fork into the bowl, spearing three of the gnocchi at once, but before I can put them into my mouth, Jeremy touches my wrist to stop me.

"Slow down," he says. "You want to taste this, right? Like, really taste it. So you have to take it one at a time. Put the dumpling in your mouth and let the butter roll over your tongue. Chew slowly, taking note of how the different flavors have come together. What does it smell like, taste like? What does it *feel* like?"

Forget smell, taste, and texture—it's the sound of his voice I'm focused on. The heat of his breath falling softly on my cheek. I push the gnocchi off of my fork and re-spear a single dumpling. Jeremy watches as I slip it through my lips, and I swear, I have never been so turned on by anything in my whole life.

Who knew the potato could be so erotic?

I chew slowly, as I have been told to, trying not to watch Jeremy watching me eat. My body floods with warmth as my taste buds target a piece of frizzled sage, the flavor of which seems to pop in my mouth.

"Whoa," I say.

"Yeah," he says.

I take a second gnocchi, this one covered in flakes of the fresh-grated Parmesan, and notice the subtle tang the cheese gives to our light, fluffy dumplings.

"So," Jeremy says, "does it beat a bacon double cheese-burger?"

"I don't know about that," I answer. "But hot damn, this is some good gnocchi."

He laughs then, a big, rolling laugh that sucks me in like a hug. I place my fork gently in the bowl, take a step closer to Jeremy and let my hands reach up to cradle his neck.

"Stella," he says. The way he says it makes my name sound buttery, like our sauce.

"Jeremy," I say back, my hands reaching up a bit, behind his ears.

He sighs lightly but doesn't pull away. He won't look me in the eye, either. Instead, he fingers a tight corkscrew of a curl that's formed at my temple.

"This is new," he says. He smooths it straight and then lets it bounce back.

"Yeah," I said. "It's going to rain tomorrow."

"It's not supposed to rain until the weekend." ·

"The hair never lies."

I stretch on my tippy-toes, bringing my face just inches from his. And for a second, I think he's going to kiss me. I feel him moving closer and closer and closer until—

He stops.

Strong hands remove mine from his neck, and Jeremy turns away.

"You eat," he says. "I'll clean up."

But just like that, my appetite is gone.

We don't talk about the almost-kiss. Not in the Kitchen, not on the ride home, and not when Jeremy says he'll see me "around." If I wasn't quite so numb from the shock of it all, I'd probably be crying.

"Hey, you," Mom says as I walk through the door.

Her voice makes me jump. "You're here!"

"You sound surprised."

"I am," I say. "You ran out of the Kitchen so fast I kind of assumed you had a date with the wine guy."

Mom grimaces. "Vince, his name is Vince. Please stop calling him the wine guy. And no, we didn't have plans."

I nod.

"But someone had plans, didn't they?" she muses.

An instant blush sprouts on my cheeks.

"I told you I needed help," I explain. "With my review? Jeremy was helping me with my review."

Mom gives me a knowing smile, her eyes crinkled in laughter. I start babbling on about the gnocchi-making session—leaving out the part about trying to get Jeremy to kiss me, that is.

"My little girl," she says, beaming. "Look how your palate is expanding!"

"Don't get any ideas," I warn. "This doesn't mean I'm going to get all hot for sushi now."

"We'll see."

I go into the kitchen to grab a glass of Diet Coke; Mom shuffles in behind me.

"So how's Max doing?" she asks, playing it casual. "I haven't seen him around in a while."

"He's still sick," I say, "and stop fishing."

"Fishing?"

"For information. About Max."

"What?" she says, maintaining faux innocence. "Is it so wrong to want to know what's going on in my daughter's life?"

"Why don't you ask me what you really want to know?"

"And what is it you think I really want to know?"

I take a swig of soda. Then I call her bluff. "You want to know if there's something going on between me and Jeremy."

Without breaking eye contact, my mother says, "*Is* there something going on between you and Jeremy?"

"No."

When I fail to elaborate, Mom presses on. "Do you *want* something to be going on between you and Jeremy?"

I shrug. "Max and I are still together."

"That's not what I asked you."

My skin begins to itch; I'm not used to having this kind of conversation with my mother. Then again, I've never crushed on someone this close to home, so to speak.

"I know you don't like to talk to me about boys," Mom continues. "I've always respected that. But Jeremy's not exactly a boy, is he?"

"I'll be eighteen in three days," I remind her.

"You're as stubborn as your father," she says. "Just . . . be careful, Stella. Okay?"

I attempt to divert her attention. "So if you didn't have a date with Vince, why did you rush out of the Kitchen so fast tonight?"

A small frown forms on Mom's lips. "I had to talk to your dad."

Not the answer I'm expecting.

"And why couldn't you do this at the Kitchen?" I ask.

She sighs. "I wanted a little privacy. Is that okay with you?"

Her voice turned prickly so quickly that my curiosity is instantly piqued. "Why would you need privacy to talk to *Dad*?"

She sighs again. "Come on. Let's go sit in the living room."

This sounds serious. Feeling even itchier than I did

before, I follow Mom out to the couch, and before her butt even hits the cushion I say, "What's wrong? Is he sick or something? Are you?"

Mom dismisses this idea with a wave of her hand. "No, nothing like that."

"Then what? You're kind of freaking me out."

"Stella, calm down. I just . . . I wanted to tell him about Vincent. That's all."

"Oh," I say, feeling slightly relieved. "How did he react?"

"He said he was happy for me."

"That's good, I guess. So did you . . ."

"What?" she says. "Ask him about Masha?"

I nod.

"No. And he didn't volunteer anything, either. So I guess he's not ready to discuss it with either of us."

"Huh."

I mull this over a bit, trying to figure out why Dad would keep Masha a secret from Mom, especially now that he knows I'm on to him.

"What's going on between you and your dad, anyway? He was asking me a ton of questions about you and your internship. I got the feeling you haven't talked to him much lately."

I instantly feel defensive, so I rat Dad out and tell Mom about all the unanswered messages, and how long it took him to return my call.

She frowns. "That doesn't sound like your dad."

"Tell me about it."

Mom sighs. "I hate to say it, but you're going to have

to take the high road on this one. Promise me you'll call him before Saturday. It would be best if we could minimize the drama for your party."

"Drama? What drama?"

"Here's the thing," Mom says. "The reason I wanted to tell your dad about me and Vince is because . . . well, Stella, I'd like you to get to know Vince."

"Um, okay."

"So in the spirit of getting to know one another," she continues, "I sort of invited Vince to your birthday dinner on Saturday."

"Sort of, or did?"

"Did."

Unbelievable.

"You're going to make Dad cook for the wine guy?" I ask.

"I'm not *making* your dad do anything," she says. "He knows Vince is going to be there. That's part of what we were talking about tonight."

"I don't care if he knows," I say. "It's still twisted."

"I'm sorry you feel that way."

What I feel is irritated. It's bad enough that Mom invited her new boyfriend to my birthday party. But the fact that she asked Dad's permission and not mine seems totally unacceptable.

"You're mad at me," she says.

"Yeah, actually. I am."

"What can I do to make it up to you?"

"I suppose uninviting him is out of the question?"

"Yes."

"Then never mind."

"I think I'm going to turn in early tonight. It's been a long day." Mom leans over and kisses my forehead before going off to bed.

I go to bed, too, but I find myself lying in the dark, eyes wide open, trying to quiet the noise in my brain. I'm not sure how I feel about this "getting to know the wine guy" business, but it seems so important to Mom. Plus at least she's *trying*. Dad had the perfect opportunity to come clean about him and Masha tonight, and he still didn't say anything. What does that mean? That they're not really serious? That it's already over?

And of course, there's another unanswered question I keep coming back to:

Why did Jeremy turn away?

"Gee, think they like chicken around here?"

Patricia Mascitti sniffs the air, waffling between a soup/salad combo and the hot lunch option. As she debates, I tell the caf lady I'll take the chicken parm.

"Yeah, okay," Pat says. "I'll have that, too. No, wait— I'll have the sandwich. Yeah, definitely the sandwich."

We head over to a small table in the corner. Well, I head over. Pat lingers at the drinks fridge. I've got my usual Diet Coke; a few minutes later, Pat finally joins me, her tray bearing a decaf iced tea and a bottle of skim milk.

"Do you always have trouble deciding what to order?" I ask. "Or is that a pregnancy thing?"

"Well," she says, "the pregnancy's made it harder, but

no, it always takes me forever to figure out what I want to eat. I mean, I love food. *Love* it. The catering for my wedding cost seven times everything else combined—and no, that's not an exaggeration. I even *dream* in menus. I figure since you can only eat three meals a day—well, if you want to stay a reasonable size, that is—you've got to really *feel* what you're eating, right?"

Spoken like a true foodie. I fight the urge to groan. Instead, I say, "Sometimes my mom will get angry at her stomach, because it gets full before her mouth does."

Pat laughs. "Yes, exactly."

She peels the plastic cap off her milk and drains the bottle in one long gulp. Then, without so much as a pause, she takes a humongous bite of her sandwich. A bit of mayo squirts out the bottom and lands on her chest.

"Oh, jeez," she says, wiping at it with her napkin. "The bigger my boobs get, the more food they collect."

I squirm a little, not really wanting to talk about Patricia Mascitti's boobs—or any of her other body parts, for that matter.

"Sorry," she says. "My internal filter seems to be dying a quick death. Anyway, there's a reason I asked you to lunch today."

"I figured."

Pat takes another mouth-busting bite of sandwich, and I wait for her to finish chewing.

"Mostly I want to know how you're doing," she says finally. "I know Mike threw a lot at you, what with the review column and everything. Have you seen the logo, by the way? It's gorgeous. Speaking of, Abby—the photo editor?—wanted me to remind you that she needs a head shot of you ASAP."

"Head shot?" I echo.

Pat nods vigorously. "Mike told you what they're calling the column, right? 'What's Cooking with Stella Madison?' People will want to know who you are, hence the picture."

"Oh," I say. "I didn't know. I mean, yeah, I knew the name, but not about the picture."

I push away the plate of chicken parm, feeling like I'm about to puke. It's not that I hate having my picture taken or anything. It's just that writing this review has been scary enough. To find out that my picture will be running next to it makes me feel . . . I don't know. Exposed?

"We're running an extended bio with the first review," Pat chatters. "It's got a bit about your parents. You'll get to see it this afternoon, before it goes to print."

Even better!

"You look unhappy," Pat remarks.

"Sorry," I mumble. "It's just that—"

"I think I get it," she interrupts. "You don't want people thinking you got this job because of who your parents are."

"Except that's exactly why I got this job, isn't it?"

Pat chews thoughtfully. "I guess you could look at it that way. Or you could look at it like 'My parents helped me get my foot in the door, but my talent got me an invitation to stay.' "

She opens her bag of Ruffles and offers me some. I take one, Pat takes one, and we crunch in unison. After another round of chips, she says, "Look, Stella. I have to be honest. I was kind of surprised when you accepted this job. I mean, I've seen you at the Kitchen. You don't eat, except when your dad's cooking, and even then, there's always stuff left on your plate. I know food isn't your thing. But Mike had me read your clips, and they're good. The one about the school mascot had me laughing out loud."

"I didn't come up with that idea. It was assigned to me."

"So?" she says. "You wrote it, didn't you? At any rate, I'm glad you're here."

"Really?"

"Yeah," she says. "It's okay that you're not into food, you know. Take this experience for what it is: an excellent opportunity to make some money while building your portfolio. Then, if you want to do another internship next summer, it won't have to be here. In fact, the *Baltimore Sun*'s got a great program with a features-writing track."

Pat buries her face back in her sandwich, and I chew over her words. When it came to my job at the *Journal*, I mostly focused on the money part—at first, anyway. But even after my Mrs. Banderas revelation and my resolve to kick ass this summer, I haven't really thought about what I'll do next. I mean, yes, Jeremy and I talked about me writing for a music magazine, but that was just talk. Wasn't it?

After washing down the rest of her sandwich with the iced tea, Pat asks me how my review of Morte di Fame is coming.

"It's coming," I say. "I've been rewriting all morning."

"Don't overthink it," she advises. "Write it like you're having a conversation with someone. Your dad, maybe."

I nod.

Pat reminds me that Mike needs the column by two and tells me that if I need any last-minute help I should come see her. Then she says, "I was thinking, you should probably eat at Sel de Mer before you interview Saffron Bell tomorrow. Damn, we could've had lunch there on the paper. Oh, well. Let me get you some petty cash so you're covered for dinner."

Back at my desk, I reread my revision (still terrible!), and open a fresh Word doc. The blank white page stares back at me, taunting me with its emptiness. Why did Jeremy think eating frizzled sage would help me write a decent restaurant review?

Then I hear Pat's words echoing in my head. No overthinking. Conversational writing.

I slam the rest of my Diet Coke, and shutting off my own internal filter, I start typing my new-and-improved write-up of Morte di Fame:

> Here are a few words of friendly advice for executive head chef Gordon Jenkins of Delaware Avenue's newish Morte di Fame: if you're going to open an Italian restaurant in the space formerly occupied by Wilmington's beloved seafood paradise, Deep Blue, it might be a good idea to (a) hire a decorator who knows the downtown scene, (b) train your staff to have some sort of competency, and (c) serve food deserving of the "gourmet" label you so capriciously give it.

I read it over a few times. It's not bad. I'm particularly proud of the bit about Deep Blue, though I wouldn't have known that about the location if Enrique hadn't gone on and on about it for weeks.

Feeling slightly more emboldened, I go through my notes from the other night and try to really let loose. The words pour out of me at a feverish pace. I talk about how all three kinds of bruschetta were served cold, how gluey the gnocchi were, how the swordfish tasted fishy instead of citrusy, and how even the dessert I ordered—the blood-orange torte with mascarpone cream—tasted a lot like bitter Jell-O in soggy pie crust topped with half-melted Cool Whip.

I end it with this:

> I might've been able to overlook the uncomfortable chairs if it hadn't taken the hostess a full fifteen minutes to seat us in them, even though the restaurant was at a third of capacity and the bar almost completely empty. I might've been able to overlook the lipstick print that appeared on my dining companion's "fresh" glass of water if it hadn't taken our largely uninterested waiter nearly half an hour to replace it. And I might've been able to overlook the uninspired, poorly prepared dishes if it hadn't taken a pit stop at the nearest Burger King directly after "dinner" to make me feel satisfied.
>
> So here are my words of advice to you: skip Morte di Fame. You'll have a better experience at the local Olive Garden.

I'm typing that last sentence when I feel my Sidekick vibrate against my thigh. I click Save and answer the call. It's Max.

"Guess who's feeling human?" he says by way of a greeting.

"Um, I don't know," I say. "Could it possibly be you?"

My tone is teasing, but instantly my muscles tighten. One good thing about Max being sick is that I haven't really had to deal with him all that much. I feel guilty even thinking that, but it's true. This past week has been confusing enough without the pressure of Max's declarations of love and the guilt I feel almost every time I return them.

"Let's do something tonight," Max says. His voice is no longer nasal, and there's a brightness to it that makes me smile despite myself.

I tell him I'm supposed to have dinner at Sel de Mer. Then, realizing I don't have a dining companion lined up, I ask him if he'd like to go with me.

"Hells yeah!" he says. "When should I pick you up?"

"How about six-thirty?"

"Awesome! Can't wait to see you."

"Me too," I say, even though I'm pretty sure I don't mean it.

The minute Max hangs up, I'm tempted to dial Kat. Then I remember her speech about how sick she is of the "Max-Jeremy dance" and decide to call Olivia instead. Then I remember *her* speech about telling Max that I have the hots for Jeremy and realize that this time, I'm on my own.

So I dive back into my review, proofreading it and tightening the sentences the best I can. I deliver the draft to Mike Hardwick just shy of two o'clock. Then I pull up Sel de Mer's menu online so I can draft an ordering strategy like Jeremy taught me. Not half an hour later, Mike comes bounding over to my desk, an angry look on his face.

I knew I'd gone too far. Even though every single word I wrote was true, it was probably poor etiquette to slam a restaurant that could potentially advertise in the *Daily Journal*. I'm steeling myself for a pride-swallowing apology when Mike Hardwick bellows, "You are such a liar!"

"Excuse me?"

His stern face melts away and is replaced by a smiling, jovial one. "I knew you'd be brilliant at this, Stella Madison! This is the most spirited review we've had in *Snap!* You're going to have to cut a few of those adverbs you seem to love so much, but brava, my dear! And you said you couldn't do this job." He shakes his head as if to say, "Silly Stella."

Mike asks for an update on the Saffron Bell profile, and I tell him that Pat suggested I check out the restaurant tonight, as my interview's scheduled for early tomorrow.

"How early?" he asks.

"Seven."

"Damn," he says, "that *is* early. You should probably check out the car tonight, then. And feel free to cut out around two tomorrow, okay? To compensate."

"Wow," I say. "Thanks."

"This is going to be a great summer, Stella," he says, beaming. "I just knew you'd work out fine."

The weird thing?

I'm actually starting to believe him.

— 15 —

SEL DE MER

DINNER SPECIALS FOR THURSDAY, JUNE 25

Appetizer: creamy albacore couscous with caper berries
Main Course: butter-poached halibut cheeks topped with
heirloom-tomato coulis on a bed of crab-and-pea-shoot risotto
Vegetable: sautéed sunchokes and bacon
Dessert: roasted pear with Stilton and walnuts in local honey

While I'm waiting for Judy, the office manager, to process the car request, I call Mom and let her know about my dinner date.

"I think I might be jealous!" she says. "Let me know if you think I should try to get this woman on our calendar, okay? And have fun!"

"Will do."

I'm so thrilled that I don't have to take the bus that I end up driving home at a leisurely pace. I've got the windows rolled down and the radio cranked up. Bright sunshine warms my left cheek and arm, and I'm still glowing from Mike Hardwick's unexpected praise.

At home, I shrug out of my work clothes and into a particularly girly Hawaiian-print sundress. I pull my hair into a messy ponytail at the base of my neck and spritz on some honeysuckle-scented spray I got from Bath & Body Works. Watermelon-flavored lip gloss and a wristful of plastic bangles complete my look, which I've dubbed "summer personified."

Max picks me up at six-thirty sharp; the first thing I notice about him is that he's lost a significant amount of weight. So much that when he hugs me, I actually feel rib bones pressing into me.

"You look . . . thin," I say carefully.

Max snorts. "Try scrawny. I must've dropped fifteen pounds. That's what happens when you can't keep anything in your system for longer than an hour."

We climb into the car; as Max pulls away from the curb, I see that, in addition to the weight, he's also lost his gorgeous summer tan. Not to mention quite a bit of muscle tone.

"You checking out my arms?" Max says. "Don't worry. A week or two on the courts and I'll be back in fighting shape."

I'm not sure which is worse—the fact that I am apparently the evilest, shallowest girlfriend on the planet, or that my poor, sickly boyfriend condones said shallowness.

Max asks me how my day has been, and I tell him about lunch with Pat and how Mike seemed to like my second attempt at the Morte di Fame review.

"Speaking of," I say, "we need to discuss what we're going to order tonight."

"What do you mean?"

I explain the rules to him. "So I'll take the specials. I wrote down what you need to get."

"You're choosing my food for me?"

I sigh. "Max, I told you. This is an assignment."

"But what if I don't like the stuff you've picked out?"

"Order them anyway," I snap. Then, in a softer tone, I add, "If you really hate the food, I'll spring for KFC on the way home, okay?"

"Yes, ma'am," he says.

I apologize for being sharp with him. "It's just a lot of pressure," I explain. "This job, these reviews . . . I don't want to look foolish, you know?"

"Aw, Stella," he says. "You could never look foolish."

He says this in the way any good, supportive boyfriend would. But instead of feeling better, I prickle with annoyance.

"Are you psyched about your birthday?" Max asks.

"Eh," I say. "Not so much."

"Why's that?"

"Well," I say, "my mom's invited this new guy she's dating. And my dad's cooking, but I haven't talked to him in a week, and the last time I saw him he was making goo-goo eyes at Masha Tobash. You remember, that loud woman from the Food Network?"

"I take it you don't like her?"

"That's not the point!" I say.

"So what is the point?"

"My parents, Max. They're dating other people."

There's a pause. Then Max says, "I thought your parents have been separated for a long time."

"They have."

"Then I'm not sure I understand why you're so upset."

"Of course not. Your parents have been married since they were in the womb."

"Hey," Max says. "That's not fair. I want to understand."

It should be enough—"should" being the operative word.

"Forget about it," I say. "I don't want to spend the night talking about *them*. Let's have fun, okay?"

Even though it was my suggestion to drop the subject, I'm a little thrown by how quickly Max agrees.

We arrive at Sel de Mer a good ten minutes before our reservation but are seated right away. I pull the paper with Max's order out of my purse and slide it over to him.

"Order it just like I've written," I say.

"Yes, ma'am," he says again.

"Quit it."

"Quit what?"

"With the 'yes, ma'am' stuff. You make me feel like a dictator or something."

"Sorry."

Max's face morphs into that of a child who's been reprimanded one time too many. Actually, he looks a lot like Cory does whenever his mother tells him to stop climbing all over me. Instantly I regret inviting him to come with me. I can feel how awful I'm behaving, but I can't seem to stop it. The worst part is that Max hasn't done a single thing to deserve it. Except maybe fall for the wrong girl.

We place our orders; as the waitress retreats to the kitchen, Max reaches into his pocket. He pulls out a pouch full of little plastic toys.

"Check it out," he says. "They're part of my put-pocket mission."

"Your what?"

"Put-pocket. I thought it up when I was sick. I was watching a *Law & Order* rerun and the cops were chasing this murderous pickpocket dude. And suddenly I thought, you always hear about pickpockets, but you never hear about a put-pocket.

"It's genius, right?" he continues, grinning. "Instead of *taking* something from someone, you *put* something fun in their pocket. Then, when they get home at night, they're like, 'Hey, how did I end up with this pirate in my pocket?' "

"You are so weird," I say, but even as the words spill out of my mouth I feel my lips curl into a smile. "That's actually kind of adorable."

"So what do you think, Stel? Wanna be my put-pocket partner in crime?"

And just like that, I'm reminded of why I liked Max to begin with. It's not solely because he's good-looking and athletic and gets along with pretty much everyone. And it's not just because he liked me first. It's because no matter how "conventional" people like Kat think he is, there's always something surprising lurking just beneath the surface. I mean, put-pocketing—who thinks of something like that?

Max, that's who.

For the next hour or so, I'm able to let go of all of my guilt and ambivalence and actually *enjoy* being with my boyfriend. Even the food doesn't throw me, partially because Max knows even less than I do about the culinary arts, and so instead of feeling horribly inadequate, I get to play teacher. We taste each other's dishes, and even though I doubt I'll be ordering halibut cheeks anytime soon, I can tell that the fish is firm, sweet, and well-seasoned. I also know the risotto is prepared perfectly, because that's one of those things chefs love to make at the Kitchen, and they're always going on and on about the texture of the rice and its "mouth feel."

I eat slowly and take copious notes, starting to formulate questions for tomorrow's interview. Max watches appraisingly. At one point he leans in and whispers, "You make smart look really sexy," and my entire body tingles from the compliment.

Later, parked in front of my house, we kiss for at least an hour. It's all about hands and tongues and mouths, and when I finally come up for air, I'm literally breathless.

Max tucks a curl behind my ear and says, "God, I've missed you."

Automatically I reply, "Me too." Only, now, I think maybe I *do* mean it.

It's not until after we've said our goodbyes that I realize nothing's changed.

I'm still just a bubbleheaded, boy-crazy, bouncy rubber ball.

Mom gets home not long after I do, and over lemonade and oatmeal-raisin cookies Enrique whipped up special for me, I tell her about my day: the talk with Pat, Mike Hardwick's positive response to my review, even the awkward-turned-awesome date with Max.

"So things are good with Max, then?" she asks.

I shrug. "I guess so. Yeah. I like him, Mom."

"And Jeremy?"

"What about Jeremy?"

"He's planning on helping out at your party, you know."

"So?"

"So," she says, "I'm wondering if Max knows about your and Jeremy's . . . friendship."

"Stop," I say. "You make 'friendship' sound like a bad word. I don't know how many times I have to tell you that nothing is going on between me and Jeremy. Besides, shouldn't you be more worried about parading the new boyfriend around Dad?"

"Speaking of," Mom says, ignoring my prickly question, "have you gotten ahold of your father yet?"

My silence answers for me.

"Stella," Mom chastises. "Your party is in two days. Promise me you'll take care of this tomorrow."

"I'll do my best."

"Stella . . ."

"Fine!" I exclaim. "I'll call him tomorrow, okay?"

I feign tiredness and excuse myself, reminding Mom that I've got an early morning ahead. But sleep doesn't come easily. I replay the events of the evening like they're on a closed-loop circuit, each time growing more confused as to how tiny plastic pirates could turn bitchy annoyance into steamy affection almost instantaneously. I mean, really. What kind of person am I, anyway?

I finally pass out around three a.m., but when my alarm goes off at five-thirty I'm convinced that I've only just fallen into slumber. After pressing Snooze three times, I realize if I don't haul myself out of bed I'm going to be late.

Between rushing to get ready and tamping down the nervousness about my early-morning interview with Saffron Bell, I almost—*almost*—forget that "What's Cooking with Stella Madison?" debuts in today's paper. In fact, I'm much more concerned with the humidity level and whether or not I can get away with liquid foundation than I am any journalistic endeavors. I decide to go with a tinted moisturizer and am just about to smooth some on my face when I hear my mother shrieking.

I tear out of my room; Mom's in the kitchen, leaning over the counter. For a minute, I think she's chopped a finger off or something.

"What is it?" I say. "Are you hurt? Do you need stitches?"

Mom whips around, looking slightly manic as well as confused. "What? No, I'm fine. But look!"

She holds up the front page of the *Journal*—the front page of the *entire paper*—and I see what's made my mom scream.

It's a teaser for my column, top of the fold, just under the dateline.

"Oh, my god," I say. "Oh. My. *God*."

"I know, right?" Mom gushes, sounding more like me and my friends than her usually articulate self. "Now look!"

She thrusts the *Snap!* section at me, opened to page three, where my column appears. The first thing I notice—besides my byline, of course—is the black-and-white headshot Abby took yesterday. Thank god for the miracle that is Photoshop; the picture's been retouched to make my hair look softly curly, not the hotbed of frizz I know it was by the afternoon. Also, I'm pretty sure Abby took out the dark circles under my eyes, but it's such a small shot that I can't be certain.

" 'Better experience at the Olive Garden,' " Mom says, repeating my own review back to me. She's grinning so hard I'm afraid her face is going to split in half. "Oh, Stel. This is so good! Granted, you probably just cost me a bunch of sales at the Kitchen—Gordon's scheduled for two nights next month, if you remember—but oh, it's *so* good, Stella, I can't even be upset. I'm so proud of you!"

She pulls me into a Mama Bear hug so tight I can barely breathe. Then she says, "Did you know you'd be on the front page? Enrique's going to *die*. You better bring me home a bunch of extra copies. At least a dozen. No! Make it two. And who would I talk to about getting extra *Snap!* inserts delivered to the Kitchen?"

I tell her I don't know but I'll find out this afternoon.

"You'll bring me extras, though, right?"

"Yes, Mom," I say, pretending to be annoyed but secretly loving the fuss. "Now I have to go get ready or I'll be late for my interview."

"Yes, yes, of course. Go get ready, my brilliant restaurant reviewer. Your father is going to be tickled, just tickled."

I arrive at Sel de Mer a full fifteen minutes early, but the door is already open. Inside, I find Saffron Bell

— 184 —

waiting for me with two cups of espresso and a tray of miniature croissants.

"I figured you'd be hungry," she says, extending her hand. "Hi, I'm Saffron."

"Stella," I say. "And wow—thanks for the treats."

Her intensely blue eyes sparkle as she says, "Well, I figured I better be nice to you or else you'd give me the Gordon Jenkins treatment."

I must've pulled a face or something, because Saffron says, "I'm totally kidding. I've eaten at Morte di Fame, and your review was spot-on."

"Um, thanks." Still, I suddenly feel really naked. It's one thing to have your mom reference something you wrote; it's entirely another to know some stranger has ingested your words and now fears you because of them.

"Can we, um, get started?"

Saffron nods. "Absolutely."

Since I've already researched her resume and eaten at her restaurant, I skip the usual background questions and go straight for the meat.

"So, um, do you feel like you inherited your culinary point of view from your mentor, or is it something you crafted yourself?"

"Wow, okay," she says. "Probably a bit of both, actually. I feel like when Robert took me on, I was just learning to crawl, and by the time I left, I could walk. Now, having my own place . . . it's like being able to run a marathon."

"Nice metaphors," I say.

"Why, thank you."

With the first question out of the way, I feel my stiffened body relax a bit. I even eat one of the yummy pastries, which are still warm. We talk about what it's like to be young and female and how that's affected her career. We talk about the cultural differences between Vancouver and Wilmington. We even talk about what she'd order if she was stranded on a desert island that only had Burger Kings.

We laugh a lot, too—partially because of my "out there" questions (like the BK one) and partially because Saffron's just really, really funny. She's tiny and moves like a dancer—I tell her that when she walks she reminds me of seaweed underwater, to which she replies, "You totally need to print that"—but she's also really solid, too. Confident. Sure of herself. Her sapphire blue eyes are piercing when she speaks, because she never breaks contact and because she never doubts a word that comes out of her mouth. Or at least, that's how it seems.

Ninety minutes later, I find myself shaking hands with her again. "Thanks for the great interview," I say.

"No," she says, "thank *you*. This was fun."

Actually, it *was* fun. Really fun. Who would've thought that I, Stella Madison, could get so much enjoyment out of talking to someone about food?

Here's something else I never would've guessed about myself: I'm kind of good at this food-writing thing.

By the time I get into the office at ten a.m., Mike Hardwick had already fielded a dozen or so phone calls about my scathing indictment of Morte di Fame. One angry—Gordon Jenkins, naturally—but the rest over-whelmingly complimentary. The most-cited comment? "Hilarious."

Me! Hilarious!

I start to write up my profile of Saffron Bell. I'm so absorbed in this task that it's nearly one before I even look up from my computer screen. To quiet my rumbling stomach, I grab a bag of Doritos and a Diet Coke from the vending machines and get back to work. Before I leave for the day, I've finished a full draft, which I place on Mike Hardwick's desk with a satisfying thump.

As I head out, Pat Mascitti walks by and gives me a high five.

"I knew you had it in you," she says, beaming. "Now, let's see what you serve up for the next course."

— 16 —

On Saturday my mother wakes me up at the ungodly hour of eight a.m. by singing me her special birthday song, a ditty she picked up during her years at summer camp that ends with the line "Granny, cut your toenails, you're ripping the sheets—cha!" It's beyond silly, but my birthday never feels like my birthday until she sings me that stupid song.

"Happy eighteenth, sweets," she says, kissing my forehead. "Now, I've been instructed to make sure you're dressed and ready to go within the next half hour."

"By whom?"

"Kat and Olivia. They've got some big day planned. Oh, and you're supposed to pack your bathing suit."

"Gotcha."

While I'm getting ready, Max calls to give me his birthday wishes and to firm up plans for tonight. "See you at six?"

"I can't wait," I say, wishing I meant it.

My surprise "big day" begins at McDonald's, where the girls buy me breakfast. This is actually a rare treat, as I'm a total Sausage & Egg McMuffin groupie and neither

Kat nor Liv likes to hit their daily fat-gram limit over one greasy sandwich. Both give me their hash brown patties and watch in horror as I slather them in ketchup and suck them down one after the other.

"It amazes me," Kat says, "how you can eat so poorly and still have a relatively normal figure."

I shrug. "I eat when I'm hungry and stop when I'm full."

"Yeah, but think about what you're full of," Olivia says.

"Shut it," I say. "It's my birthday and I'll eat what I want to."

"She's right," Kat chimes in. "There are no calories on your birthday."

The girls give me my presents right there in the booth, saying I'll need them for tonight. Olivia's gift is a boob-hugging turquoise silk tee with cap sleeves, and Kat's is a stunning silver-and-gemstone lariat necklace with matching earrings and a hammered silver cuff bracelet of her own design.

"Look inside the bracelet," she instructs.

I do. There's an inscription that reads, "For Stella on her 18th birthday, with love from Kat (KSO-4-EVA)"— "KSO" being her shorthand for the three of us.

"I love it," I tell her, choking up a bit. "I love all of it. Thanks, you guys. Seriously, I feel so spoiled."

We spend the rest of the morning and most of the afternoon hanging out at Kat's pool. I'm in the water more than I am out of it, not caring how the chlorine will affect the texture of my curls. I swim laps, trying to block out thoughts about my parents and their respective love interests, not to mention the impending doom I feel about tonight's party. Dad in the same room with Vince? Max in the same room with Jeremy? Me in the same room with all of them at the exact same time?

When my skin has shriveled to beyond pruney, I finally haul myself out of the pool and sink into my lounge chair.

"SPF?" Kat offers.

"No thanks," I reply. "I've decided that a slow and painful death from skin cancer is really the only way to go."

"Not funny," Olivia objects. "Butter up, birthday girl."

I sigh and reluctantly take the tube of sunscreen from Kat. Its smell reminds me of Omar's backyard and the party Jeremy ended up accompanying us to. I remember how flirty he was then, how he pulled me in next to him, roasting marshmallows for both of us and then feeding me the ooey, sticky goodness himself. It was the closest I'd ever come to finding food sexy. Until the night we made gnocchi, that is.

Made gnocchi. It sounds like a cheesy euphemism for sex. The thought of this makes me giggle, which prompts Kat to ask me what's got me giggling all of a sudden. I tell her and she laughs, too. Then she says, "Hey, Liv, have you and Omar made gnocchi yet?"

Liv groans. "I am not dignifying that with a response."

"Come on, Olivia," I say. "Don't hold out."

"You know I'm not into kissing and telling," Liv shoots back.

"Whatever," Kat says. She pulls a bottle of polish out of her bag and starts to paint her toes a deep crimson.

Kat's an expert with the stuff; not a drop strays from a single nail, not even the one on her baby toe.

At three, Liv and I pack up our stuff and head back to my place. As she drops me off, Liv says, "Do me a favor, Stella?"

"What?"

"Try to have fun tonight," she says. "I know you're pissed at your dad and bummed about all this dating drama, but you only get your eighteenth birthday once. And look it at this way—as of today, you can legally purchase porn!"

I laugh. "As opposed to when I used to buy it illegally?"

"Okay, so no porn. What about lotto tickets?"

"Goodbye, Liv."

I shower, dress, and run a little styling cream through my superdry hair. (Damn that chlorine!) Makeup is kept to a minimum; I forgot to apply the sunscreen to my face and now have mild sunburn across my cheeks and nose. Kat will be horrified, but I have to admit, I think it looks kind of cute. It's even brought out a smattering of sun freckles, or as Kat calls them, "death dots."

As I sit on the couch, waiting for Max to pick me up, I touch the cuff bracelet Kat made me, admiring how the silver glows against Olivia's silk shirt. I realize that an awful lot of people have gone to an awful lot of trouble just to help me celebrate my birthday tonight. I'm hit by a wave of guilt over how selfish I've been. I didn't even keep my promise to Mom and call Dad yesterday like I said I would. Feeling chastened, I vow to take Liv's advice about tonight.

Max arrives just before six.

"Wow," he says, giving me the up-down. "You look fantastic."

"Thanks." I feel myself blush under the sunburn. "Should we go?"

"Just a sec." He reaches into the pocket of his chinos and pulls out a small pale blue box with a white ribbon tied around it. "I know you're not big into mush, so I figured I better give you this here instead of in front of everyone else. Happy birthday, Stella." He leans in and kisses my cheek.

Slowly I untie the ribbon and place it on a nearby end table. With a lump forming in my throat, I take the top off the box. Inside rests a ring with a small pink pearl sandwiched between two tiny diamond chips.

I gasp. "It's beautiful," I say. "But oh, my god, it's too much, Max. I can't—"

"Before you freak, you should know it's not *actually* from Tiffany. I found it at an estate sale my mom dragged me to earlier this summer. It's like, used. Or antiqued. Whatever. My mom says that it's bad luck for women to buy themselves pearls, so . . ."

"I can't," I say again.

"Sure you can." Max plucks the ring from inside the box and gently slips it onto the appropriate finger of my right hand. "See? Perfect fit."

At least he didn't go for the left hand, I think.

"I don't know what to say."

Max smiles and squeezes my now ring-adorned hand. "You don't have to say anything. Let's go get our cake on, okay?"

Wordlessly, I follow him out the door, wondering what exactly I've gotten myself into.

THE OPEN KITCHEN
MENU FOR SATURDAY, JUNE 27
Chef André Madison of Mélange
** CLOSED FOR PRIVATE PARTY **

By the time we arrive, the Kitchen is packed and the punch is flowing. From the minute Max and I walk through the door—hand in hand, of course—I smell an intoxicating combination of my favorite foods: the chicken fingers my dad made for me when I was little, using crushed Cap'n Crunch for the coating; Mom's famous deviled eggs; a huge bubbling pot of Ball Park franks 'n' beans. I close my eyes and breathe it all in, knowing even as I do that this is some kind of collective peace offering from my parents. Of course, it would just have to come in the form of food.

My dad is behind the counter with Jeremy, and I don't know what to feel when I see either of them. Jeremy glances up first, gives me the tiniest of winks, and returns his attention to the stovetop. My father, on the other hand, offers me a cool nod of acknowledgment, slaps his tea towel over one shoulder, and continues chopping something on a bamboo board. That's it. He greets his patrons with more enthusiasm than he does his own daughter, and on her birthday, no less.

I scan the room for my mother. She's back in the pantry area, practically swooning against a wiry-looking man with thinning reddish hair. I'm assuming this must be the infamous Vince, who in my head I pictured to be something out of *The Sopranos*, maybe on account of his name. In real life, he looks nothing like an Italian mobster. In fact, he's short, standing only an inch or two taller than my mom (who's barely five foot four); he's also pale, and seemingly devoid of any facial hair. The total opposite of my tall, scruffy-faced father.

It's definitely weird seeing my mother stand so dangerously close to the wine guy. Especially since I notice that she's actually wearing *lipstick*. Instantly I'm overcome with the same sickness I felt when I caught my dad and Masha in the hallway at Mélange: A heavy sense of dread that something is horribly askew in the universe. A golf ball in my throat blocking me from screaming, "What the hell are you doing? This is wrong, wrong, wrong!"

My eyes cut back to Dad, who's intent on whatever it is he's chopping, then sweep over to the Mom-'n'-Vince tableau. They're so into each other at the moment that neither of them has registered my arrival.

I decide to go greet my friends, most of whom I haven't seen since Omar's party. Two weeks feels more like two years. Tabitha Donnelly has already dyed her hair a new color—apple green this time around—and her look has gone from mock Goth to early-eighties punk. Jesse Carlyle is tanned and relaxed, while his older brother, Critter, is pale and twitchy. Both he and their sister, Seattle, shaved their heads last summer—no one knows why—but now his white-boy hair is sectioned off into thick cornrows, while Sea sports a cute, asymmetrical pixie cut. There's a tall hottie by her side, wearing a long black trench coat and dark glasses—totally Keanu circa *The Matrix*.

After I've made the rounds, I notice that Jeremy's dumping a huge mass of straight orange macaroni into a large glass bowl. Instantly I make a beeline in his direction.

"Is that . . . is that *Kraft*?" I ask incredulously.

"Your favorite, right?"

"*Duh*," I say. "But do my parents know you're making this?"

"It was your dad's idea."

At the mention of himself, Dad looks up at me and offers one of those uncomfortable grimaces masquerading as a half smile. Regardless of my father's odd body language, now I *know* they're trying to buy me off. Boxed mac-and-cheese is like my dad's idea of hell. For years he's tried to get me to eat the baked stuff with Japanese bread-crumb topping, but his version is way too froufrou for *moi*.

Dad heads out front and still he doesn't say a word. I'm wondering if I should follow him when Jeremy says, "You should check out the rest of the spread. I think you'll be pleased."

Just then I feel a warm hand on my shoulder. It's Max, standing slightly behind me and only inches away from Jeremy. Instantly I stiffen—even more so when Max delivers a light kiss to the back of my neck.

"Max, hey," I say, my voice quavering slightly. "Max,

this is Jeremy. He's Mom's new intern I told you about? Jeremy, this is, um, Max."

The guys shake hands, and on the outside everything seems perfectly normal. On the inside, though, I'm a hotbed of anxiety. What must Jeremy be thinking? Can Max sense how I feel? What's the quickest way I can insert the greatest amount of distance between the two of them?

Suddenly *she* emerges from the bathroom. Masha Tobash, clad in a too-fancy dress, wearing more makeup than Fergie, her dyed red hair pulled back so severely that it's giving her an instant face-lift.

"What's she doing here?" I hiss.

"Take a deep breath," Jeremy says in a low voice. "This is your night; don't let Masha make you miserable, okay?"

It's a little late for that.

"Stella!" Masha says, sauntering over to me. She does her normal double-cheek kiss thing and I get a big whiff of all her smells: some sort of Asian floral perfume, hair spray that clearly came from an aerosol can, and minty-fresh toothpaste. Not an appealing combination by anyone's standards.

"Hello, Marsha," I say, deliberately reinserting the "r." "I didn't know you were on the guest list. What a great . . . surprise."

I flash a smile, but it's chilly and insincere. And if the slightly sour look on Masha's face is any indication, she knows.

"Yes, well," she says. "Your father thought—"

"I'm sure he did."

We stand there, eyes locked. Masha's the first to look away, and when she does, I see her face turn a shade of tomato. She excuses herself and heads out the front door, and I'm guessing she'll glue herself to my father's side.

Jeremy shakes his head disapprovingly. "Play nice, Stella. No need to add to the drama, you know?"

"What drama?" Max asks.

"That's her," I explain. "My dad's girlfriend."

"Remind me why you don't like her?"

Frustrated, I ignore Max's question and instead search Jeremy's eyes for some kind of reassurance. *He* gets it. *He* understands.

"I should go say hi to Mom," I mumble, extricating myself.

This means having to greet Vince, as the two of them are sort of cooped up in one corner of the room.

Vince offers me a hand before I can say a single word. "Hi, Stella," he says. "I'm Vincent. Great review in yesterday's paper. Really choice. Oh, and, uh, happy birthday, by the way."

I know I should say something nice in return—a simple thanks, even—but instead I turn to my mother and say, "Can I steal you for a second?"

She and Vince exchange a quick glance. "Sure."

I drag her through the Kitchen and out the back door so that we can have a modicum of privacy.

"Did you know he was bringing her?" I demand.

"Absolutely not," Mom replies without me having to clarify who the "he" and "her" are. "You know me better than that. If your dad had told me that Masha was coming, I would've prepared you."

I sigh a deep, heavy sigh. "Okay. That's all I wanted to know."

"You going to be okay?"

Shrugging, I say, "What choice do I have?"

"Try to enjoy yourself," Mom says. She plants a kiss on my forehead. "You look really lovely tonight." Then, before I can even thank her for the compliment, she spies the pearl ring on my right hand. "Stella, what is that?"

"It's a ring," I say. "From Max."

"You aren't keeping it, are you?"

"I already tried to give it back. He won't take it."

Now it's Mom's turn to sigh. "Stella, you give me *agita*. Come on, let's get back to your party. We'll talk more about this later."

Inside, I find my father holding court behind the island counter. He's telling a rapt crowd about one of his first culinary apprenticeships in France, and how whenever he or another cook would make a mistake, the head chef would reprimand them by flicking their wrist or neck with the point of a sharp knife. He pulls up one sleeve on his chef's coat and shows the front row his collection of quarter-inch scars. They *ooh* and *ahh* appropriately in response.

"Hey, André," I hear Kat call out. "Tell the one about your butchering exam!"

Dad waves her off, pretending he's not completely tickled to recount this story for the umpteenth time. Masha stands off to his left, leaning against the wall and making moon eyes at him while daintily sipping a glass of white wine. I can't help thinking she looks a bit like a groupie.

My father launches into the lurid tale of a crazy culinary instructor who was so hard-core that to pass his class each student was required to butcher a spring lamb head to toe, *blindfolded*, and while doing so had to explain in excruciating detail how they'd prepare each cut of meat— original recipes only.

Normally I enjoy my father's storytelling as much as anyone else, if not more. Tonight, though, the sound of his voice gnaws at this ugly place inside of me, and I have to fight the urge to scream, "Shut up already!"

Mom must sense my irritation, because she cuts Dad off from launching into another one of his famous yarns by putting out a stack of plates and telling everyone to eat up. I don't have much of an appetite left, but I still take a greedy helping of the mac-and-cheese, a generous portion of the franks 'n' beans, a bunch of chicken fingers, and a few of the deviled eggs. Kat's got a table set up for the core crew: Max and me, Olivia and Omar, and her. I'm to sit at the head and put on a sparkly birthday tiara, which I do. Then, before I dig in, I get back up and go over to Jeremy.

"Come eat with us?" I ask.

"Can't," he says. "Technically I'm on the clock. Besides, I don't know how Max would feel about that. Nice ring, by the way."

Without a word, I turn on my heel and retreat to our table.

"What was that about?" Kat whispers, but I wave her off.

I'm so miserable at this point that I can't even enjoy my mac-and-cheese. Max keeps squeezing my knee and asking me if I'm okay, but every ounce of concern from him makes me feel even more aggravated.

"Hey, Omar," I stage-whisper across the table. "I dare you to go in the pantry and filch a bottle of rum."

Omar looks like he's considering this when Olivia jumps in and says, "Uh-uh. No deal."

"Come on, Liv," I say. "It's my birthday. Besides, this punch sucks."

Max looks at me strangely, like he's trying to figure out if I'm actually me or some android trying to pass herself off as Stella.

"What?" I say.

"You don't drink," he reminds me.

"I don't drink at high school parties," I clarify. "This is my mom's place. I know nobody's going to slip something scary into my drink here." I look around at my friends. "Come on, someone needs to be brave."

"I don't think this is a good idea," Kat says.

"Pooper," I reply. I know I sound more like eight than eighteen, but I don't care. "Fine, losers, I'll do it myself."

I make like I'm heading to the bathroom and instead slip into the pantry, where I find a small bottle of Captain Morgan next to three different kinds of sherry and some Scotch. I tuck it into the waistband of my skirt before actually going into the bathroom for some authenticity.

Although I offer my spoils to the table, I'm the only

one who adds rum to her punch. Soon, my glass is two-thirds rum to one-third punch.

Max says, "You might want to slow down," and I say, "You might want to mind your own business."

Then, like a flash, I realize that Enrique isn't here. "Where's Enrique?" I ask loudly. I stand up and repeat the question.

"Stella, shhh," Kat hisses. "Keep your voice down."

I wave her off. "It's my party, and I want my Enrique!"

As if on cue, the door opens and Enrique enters, holding Miss Sugar in his arms.

"Enrique!" I scream, running over to him and half tripping on my own feet.

He looks a bit stunned when I throw my arms around him.

"Happy birthday, babygirl," he says.

"I'm sooo glad you're here."

Enrique's nose wrinkles and he sniffs the air a bit. Then he leans in to me and says, "Have you been drinking?"

I give him my best little-girl face. "Just a little. But shhh, don't tell nobody, 'kay?"

Miss Sugar, who's wearing a pink flowered sundress and a pink silk ribbon in her hair, cowers from me as I try to plant a big, sloppy kiss on her fluffy head.

"Forget you, dog," I say, and flounce back to my table.

I notice that behind the island, my parents are standing next to each other, stirring something in a small pot. Dad whispers something in Mom's ear; she laughs a bright, tinkle of a laugh and squeezes his shoulder. Grinning in response, Dad grabs a tasting spoon from the crock, dips it into the pot, and brings it up to Mom's lips. After blowing on whatever's on the spoon, Mom takes it between her lips. She must like it; she's making that "oh, god, I'm going to die, that's so good" face.

Their respective dates stand off on the sidelines, watching them—Vince with a curious look on his face, Masha with a slightly alarmed one.

"Ha!" I say to no one in particular.

"What's up?" Liv asks.

I gesture toward my parents.

"Isn't it ironic," I say, "how 'together' they look? Especially now, when they're both screwing other people."

"Stella!" Kat exclaims, even though I've directed this last sentence to Omar.

"What?" I say. "Omar doesn't know about the wine guy. Or Masha-Marsha, for that matter."

She and Liv exchange worried looks, but I pretend to be oblivious. I empty the rest of the Captain Morgan into my glass and drink it down in one long gulp.

"That's it," Kat says. "You're flagged."

"Bullshit," I say. "I have to *pee*."

This time when I hit the pantry, I decide to smuggle out a bottle of wine. For some reason I think this is possible if I place the bottle between my knees and shuffle out to my table. I grab a partially used bottle of Grand Marnier as well and tuck it under my waistband, like I did with the rum.

I'm not sure how, but I make it to my table with both bottles intact. The wine goes directly into my bag, for later. The Grand Marnier is destined for my glass. But before I can pour myself a stiff dose, Jeremy magically appears, swiping the bottle from my hands. Recapping the top he says, "That's enough, Stella."

"Pooper," I say again, and stick my tongue out at him for good measure.

"Time for dessert!" I hear my dad call out.

I clap my hands together. "Ooh, dessert!"

Mom gets a tray from the freezer. On it is a "cake" made of slabs of vanilla ice cream sandwiched between thick layers of chocolate-covered Rice Krispie Treats. It's yet another delicacy from my childhood. I squeal when I see it and tell anyone who'll listen how yum-o the sandwiches are.

I'm drunker than I meant to get, and I feel myself wobble a bit as I make my way up to the island, where my mom is lighting a mess of tall, thin candles. Everyone launches into a chorus of the happy birthday song, and at the end I blow out all my candles in one hot breath.

"Want to know what I wished for?" I ask my parents.

"You can't tell," Max calls out from across the room. "Then your wish won't come true!"

Keeping my eyes pasted on my parents, I call back, "This one has to come true. It can't *not* come true.

"Come on, Dad," I say—the first words I've spoken directly to him all night. "Take a guess."

He shakes his head, mute.

"Mom? What about you?"

"Let's just cut the cake," she says.

I make the sound of a game show buzzer. "Time's up!

Here's what I wished for. I wished for parents who'd admit that they're still in love with one another, and not these random idiots they've started dating to make each other jealous!"

There's an audible gasp that travels around the room like an echo, and I see Mom's face blanch. My father's, however, turns red. Really red. He takes me by the arm and pulls me into the pantry.

"Ow," I say. "You're hurting me."

"What do you think you're doing? Trying to embarrass me and your mother?"

"Oh, I think you've done a pretty good job of that yourselves," I say, my words slurring together slightly. "I mean, come on, Dad. Masha Tobash? She's, like, thirty-five but wears twice as much makeup as Nana Stone!"

"You," he says, "are acting like a brat."

I wrestle my arm out of his grasp. "Fine," I say. "I'm a brat. But you—you're a liar. You lied to me, and you lied to Mom."

"What lie did I ever tell you?" he demands angrily.

"What about Masha? Okay, maybe that was more of a lie of omission—but it was still a lie."

"No. It was not."

"Yes, it was. But that's not even the worst part, is it? No, the worst part is that you left. You were married, and had a child, but you were always leaving us, weren't you? To start a restaurant, or eat and drink your way around Europe. You left, and you never once stopped to think about how that made me feel. Well, you know what? I hated it. I hated *you* for it. You're my father, and you keep leaving me, and there's no excuse for that. There just isn't."

The words come out in a torrent of tears, and when I finish I am shaking. Dad stands there, looking at me, his eyes wide and rimmed in red. I wait for him to say something—anything—but either he can't find the words or he doesn't think I deserve them.

I push past him and burst into the main room. Everybody is staring. It's too small a place for them not to have heard my tirade. Despite the rum buzz, my face burns with embarrassment. Head down, I shuffle over to where my bag is, pick it up, and ask Max if he'll drive me home. When he fails to respond, I ask Kat the same question.

"Stella—no. Just . . . just eat your ice cream sandwich, okay?"

"Fine! I'll walk!"

I rush out the door, ignoring everyone who's calling after me. Until, that is, I hear Jeremy's voice.

"Stella," he says, and I stop dead in my tracks. "Come back inside."

I shake my head.

"Stella, please."

I shake my head again.

He walks closer to me. "Come on, Stella. Calm down, okay?"

"Do you have your car keys on you?"

Jeremy frowns. "Yeah, but I'm not giving them to you. You're wasted."

"Of course," I say. "But, um, would you mind terribly taking me somewhere?"

He hesitates a beat too long, so I say, "Never mind, I'll catch a bus or something."

"But it's almost dark," Jeremy protests.

"Then drive me."

He sighs deeply, unlocks the door, and says, "Get in."

— 17 —

"So where are we going?" Jeremy asks.

"I don't care," I say. "Anywhere. Just get me out of here."

"Great."

He pulls out onto Concord Pike and heads north for a bit before turning onto Naamans Road. Jeremy drives along in silence as I stare out the window, the beginnings of a headache already settling into my frontal robe. We take a bunch of random turns until somehow we end up driving by a church carnival, complete with mile-high Ferris wheel.

"Stop the car!" I squeal. "I want to go there!"

Jeremy applies the breaks, swinging hard into a nearby 7-Eleven, busting an illegal U-turn, and rolling onto the green that's serving as the carnival's parking lot. I've got my seat belt off and am practically out of the car before he's come to a complete stop.

"I don't do rides," Jeremy warns me as I pull him through the crowd.

"No rides," I say. "Walk faster."

It doesn't take me long to find the requisite cart selling sausage and pepper sandwiches.

"Food," he says. "We came here for *food*?"

"Shhh," I tell him.

We wait in line for several minutes. When I get to the front, I order two sandwiches and two Cokes, one diet and one regular. As I fish around my bag for my wallet, Jeremy spots the bottle of wine.

"Did you steal that?" he asks.

"Shhh," I say again.

Jeremy and I find a spot under a lush elm tree, and I polish off my sandwich in about five bites.

"Isn't it divine?" I ask. "I love how the skin gets all crispy but inside it's all tender and juicy."

He cocks his head to one side. "You're one of us, you know."

"Hmm?"

"A foodie," he says.

"Am not."

"Are too. You're just a foodie about a different kind of food. Instead of haute cuisine, you wax poetic about street food."

"Whatever," I say. "Let's go."

I pull him around until I find the zeppole guy, and order two large bags of the hot, powdered-sugar-covered dough nuggets. They smell so good I bury my nose in the bag. "Heaven," I declare.

Jeremy reaches over and runs a finger over my nose. "You got sugar on it," he explains.

"Oh."

This time we wander to the far side of the church, far away from the other fairgoers, and settle into a quiet, grassy spot of our own. I take my time with the zeppole, savoring each rich, sweet bite. I offer my last one to Jeremy, who eats the nugget straight from my fingers. It's exactly the motivation I need.

I take a deep breath, then say, "I know you like me."

"Of course I like you," Jeremy says.

"No," I say. "I mean that you *like me* like me."

"I'm sorry. I didn't know we were back in junior high."

Ignoring the slight, I say, "Aren't you ever going to kiss me?"

"No," he says. "I'm not."

"Why not? It's just a kiss."

"It's never 'just a kiss.' "

Even so, our faces once again draw closer. This time, I know it's going to happen. I can feel the kiss approaching, can smell Jeremy's warm, sweet zeppole breath tickling my nose. His lips are only centimeters from mine. *Kiss, kiss, kiss*, I think.

But then he pulls away. Again.

"Damn it, Jeremy!" I say. "Why won't you kiss me? And don't you dare tell me it's because you don't want to," I continue. "Because I know you do. When we talk, you watch my mouth. You—"

"You're being awfully presumptuous," he interjects.

The lack of warmth in his tone stings harder than anything else. With a quick *pop*, I feel the air whoosh out of the helium balloon that is my heart. Hot tears begin to pool in the corners of my eyes.

Jeremy's face softens in concern. "Stella," he says, "please don't be sad."

"I'm not sad," I snap. "I'm pissed."

"Pissed?"

"You're a total tease," I accuse. "You flirt with me constantly, with the winking and the telling me how hot I am and the pulling me practically into your lap. But then, the minute I call you on it—the minute I challenge you to actually *do* something about it—you go cold.

"But you know what? No guy is worth all this drama. Not even *you*."

I'm contemplating the most graceful and dramatic exit I could make when Jeremy says, "Maybe you're right."

"About what? About you not being worth the drama?"

"That, too," he says. "But maybe you're right about the other thing as well."

"Go on."

"It's just that now . . . now isn't a good time."

"Why not?"

Jeremy sighs heavily. "Relationships," he says, "are hard."

"Yeah, and?"

"And I'm busy with classes and work, and you've got another year of high school, and if that wasn't enough, you have a boyfriend."

"A boyfriend I'm planning on breaking up with," I say.

"A boyfriend you haven't broken up with yet," he amends. He lifts my right hand and fingers the pearl ring Max gave me earlier this evening. "A boyfriend who has no idea you're about to mutilate his heart."

"What are you saying? That I'm bad girlfriend material?"

"No."

"Then what?"

Jeremy lets my hand drop. "I'm saying that relationships are hard enough without seventeen extra layers of complication. Do I like you? Yeah, Stella, I like you. I think you're hilarious. I think you're incredibly sweet and criminally cute. And I know how badly you think you want me to kiss you. But if I did, and we got involved now, the way things are? I can promise you with almost a hundred percent certainty that it would end, and end badly."

"You can't know that," I offer feebly.

"I know *myself*," he says. "And as I've told you repeatedly, it's not the right time. I'm not saying no forever, I'm just saying no for right now."

He won't look at me. I sit there, his words bouncing around my head like Ping-Pong balls: *hilarious, sweet, criminally cute*. He likes me. He likes me. And it doesn't make a damned bit of difference.

"We should go," I say. I struggle to my feet, but between the heavy food and the rum still coursing through my system, I'm woozy and stumble back down, landing hard on my ass. Then, without any warning, I promptly burst into a fresh round of tears.

Jeremy doesn't say anything, or touch me in any way. He just lets me cry. And when I eventually lean over and start sobbing into his shoulder, he doesn't stop me, opting instead to slip a long, slender arm around my back, hugging me to him.

It takes forever for me to get all cried out.

"Sorry for snotting up your shirt," I say.

"I'm sorry, too," he says. "I should've been more careful. I honestly never meant to lead you on."

" 'S'okay."

"No," he says. "It's not."

"Jeremy," I say, "in the history of the world, no girl has ever needed to be kissed as much as I do right now."

His face softens, and he smiles. "Hyperbole, anyone?"

"It's true."

I look at him, and try with my eyes to say everything I feel in my heart. And this time, when our faces draw together, there's no question that they'll meet. I feel Jeremy's hot mouth on mine even before our lips touch. My hands reach up to cup his neck; his arms circle my waist. We move together in the most natural of ways, like we've been kissing all our lives and not for the past fifteen seconds.

The kiss breaks, and I pull back. "Sorry," I say.

"Don't be."

"No," I say. "I'm sorry about *this*." Then I turn as far away from him as possible and begin to throw up.

— 18 —

There's no place left to go but home.

Jeremy hasn't said a word, save for reminding me to buckle my seat belt. I sit next to him, my window open, feeling a warm, humid breeze blow over me. I can't believe that I finally—*finally*—got Jeremy to kiss me, only to have it end in such a horrific fashion. I'm beyond mortified. Not just about throwing up, either. In addition to public drunkenness and the extreme manipulation of someone else's feelings, there's the scene I made at the Kitchen, and the terrible things I said to my father, even if they were sort of true.

Okay, entirely true.

"How are you feeling?" Jeremy asks, breaking my train of thought.

"I've been better."

"I'm sure."

Then I say, "Everyone heard, didn't they? What I said to my dad?"

"Yeah," he says. "I think so."

"Damn."

"For what it's worth, I think it's a good thing. I mean,

it would've been better if you hadn't been, you know, plastered. But it sounds like you've needed to say those things for a while."

I nod. "The weird thing is that I didn't know I needed to until I actually did."

We pull up to my house; Jeremy puts the car in park and lets it idle.

"I'm sorry I dragged you into my nightmare," I say. "But thank you. For tonight. And, well, for everything, really."

Jeremy nods. "You're going to be okay, Stella. You're stronger than you think you are."

"Tell that to my stomach."

He grins. "Go sleep it off. I promise you'll feel a hundred percent better in the morning."

I'm cloaked in dread as I take the stairs up to our town house. I can't even imagine how angry my mother is going to be, not to mention how much trouble I've gotten myself into.

So I'm surprised to walk in and find my mother curled up on the couch, her eyes as red and raw as my own.

"Hi, Mom," I say. "Are you . . . are you okay?"

She nods. "Are you?"

"I think so," I say. "I'm . . . I'm really sorry."

I can barely get the words out without breaking down yet again. The sobs engulf my entire body, and I fall to my knees, burying my head in my mother's lap. She strokes my hair.

"Oh, Stel," she says. "I had no idea."

I snuffle back the last of my tears. "Does this mean I'm not in trouble?"

"Oh, no," Mom says. "You're in so much trouble, even Trouble's like, 'Wow, that's some serious trouble.' "

I laugh despite myself.

"I can't believe you stole liquor right out from under me," she says.

"I know. I'm so sorry."

"You're going to be sorrier tomorrow," she assures me. "But right now, I think maybe what you need is a cup of tea and a good night's sleep."

"Thanks," I say, "for understanding. Or whatever."

We hug, and I shuffle off to my room. I'm so exhausted that even my bones feel tired. As I change into my pj's, I think of how many apologies I'm going to have to issue as a result of tonight's antics. And Max . . . what am I going to say to Max? I take the pearl ring off my finger and place it on my bedside table. Then I pass out the instant my head hits the pillow.

The next morning, I'm woken by the incessant beeping of my Sidekick. I've got a pounding headache and a phone full of missed calls, half a dozen of which are from Max. So even though all I really want to do is down some Advil and sleep off the hangover, instead I take several deep breaths and call him back.

He answers on the third ring.

"Hey," I say. "You have a minute?"

"What's up?"

"I want to apologize," I begin.

"For which part?" Max asks coldly. "For getting trashed and abandoning me at your birthday party? For leaving with some guy I find out you've had the hots for all summer long?"

I can feel the blood drain from my face. "Who told you that?"

"Omar," he says. "Apparently he didn't even know I was your boyfriend."

"Oh, Max," I say. "I'm so sorry."

A heavy silence grows between us.

"I'm going to give you the ring back," I offer lamely.

"Seriously?" Max says. "You think I'm worried about the ring?"

"No. I just—"

"What I want to know," Max interrupts, "is why you bothered to tell you that you love me. Because clearly you never did."

"That's not true," I say. "I thought I did. Really."

"You have a funny way of showing it."

Max has never talked to me so unkindly before. So even though I know he's justified in his anger, I'm still taken aback.

"Please," I say. "I'm trying to explain."

"So explain."

I take a deep breath and begin. "I wanted to love you. I tried to. You're the best guy I know, Max. You're so good. You were so good to *me*. But I don't know if I'm broken or whatever. I just . . . it felt like too much."

"And what about Jeremy?" he says. "Did he feel like too much?"

"Nothing happened with him," I say. It's mostly true. Telling Max about last night's kiss would only hurt him more, and that's the last thing I need to do right now.

"Doesn't matter," Max says. "You wanted something to happen. That's almost worse."

"You're right," I say. "It's way worse."

I don't know what I thought I could accomplish in a single phone call. I mean, did I really expect Max to be cool about everything? Did I really expect to walk away his friend?

And even as I think it, I realize that's exactly what I want. For us to be friends.

"I know you probably hate me right now," I say. "But Max, I honestly hope that someday you can forgive me, and maybe . . . I don't know . . ."

"I don't hate you," Max says, exasperated. "But I can't do the friend thing right now, okay?"

"Fair enough."

"I really did love you, you know," he says.

"Yeah," I say. "I know."

When I wake up for the second time that morning, it's to the sizzling smell of bacon. Curious, I pull on a robe and venture out to the kitchen, where I am surprised to see my father making what looks like his famous sweet crepes with bananas and Nutella.

"Hi, Dad," I say tentatively.

"Good morning, Stella-belle. Crepe?"

I shake my head. "I don't have much of an appetite right now."

"Nonsense," he says. "I am making bacon. Your appetite will return."

As if to prove a point, Dad lifts a piece with a pair of tongs and hands it over to me. It's hot, and the grease burns my fingertips, but I eat it anyway.

"See?" he says. "What did I tell you?"

His mood borders on jovial, which leaves me feeling uneasy. I mean, I really lit into him yesterday. Shouldn't he be dishing some of it back?

"Where's Mom?" I ask.

"She went to get some oranges. You know I won't drink juice from a carton."

"Of course."

"Go on, sit," Dad instructs. He lays out three plates, forks, napkins. Then he turns his attention back to his crepes.

"Dad, what are you doing?"

"Making crepes," he says, as if this explains everything. "When I am upset, I cook. It relaxes me. You know this."

"Yes," I say. "But what are you *doing*?"

"Your mother should be back shortly."

Dad starts loading my plate up with crepes and bacon and pours me a large mug of coffee. Next to it he places a bottle of ibuprofen.

"You will need this, too, yes?"

"What I really need," I say, "is to understand why you didn't tell me you were dating Masha Tobash."

With a heavy sigh, Dad takes a seat next to me. "You want to know why I did not tell you about Masha," he says, "but you never have asked me about any other women. There have been others, Stella."

"I'm sure there have."

"Then what is so different about Masha?"

"Because! I see how you look at her, Dad. She's not one of your . . . *women*. You like her. You like her a lot."

"Yes," he agrees. "I do."

Even though I knew this already, having him confirm it . . . well, it *hurts*.

Apparently, my poker face isn't as good as Dad's, because the next thing he says is, "I am sorry if I hurt you. It was not my intention."

"I didn't think it was," I say quietly.

"This thing with Masha—it's complicated. Her life is in New York, and my life is here. I did not say anything to you because I didn't know where our friendship would lead. I still do not know."

"Do you have other 'friends'?" I ask him.

He shakes his head. "No."

"For how long?"

"Six months. Maybe more."

"And Masha? Does *she* have other 'friends'?"

He shakes his head again.

"Dad!" I exclaim. "That's the very definition of having a girlfriend! Maybe she's a long-distance girlfriend, but she's *still a girlfriend*."

He shrugs. "I do not like labels."

"No," I say. "You don't like commitment."

Before we can get into it any further, Mom returns with a large sack of oranges. Dad immediately begins juicing them, while Mom sits next to me and starts dig-ging into her own plate of crepes, oblivious to the thick tension between me and my father.

"God, these are amazing," she says, looking like she just saw the face of Jesus himself. "André, you make the best crepes in the entire universe."

"Stop, or you will make me blush."

Dad joins us at the table. My parents continue to eat. Watching them stuff their faces, acting like nothing happened, makes me feel like I'm going to throw up again.

"Stop it!" I shout. "Stop eating! For one second, can we deal with something other than food?"

My parents exchange looks and then, at the exact same moment, start to laugh.

"What? What's so funny?"

"We're not dealing with food," Mom says. "Food's how we deal with the other stuff."

"Huh?"

Dad says, "I am not so good with words. But give me an egg. Give me some butter. I speak through my food."

"It's like how you and I can have an entire conversation without talking," Mom cuts in. "I can read your eyebrows, your smiles. With me and your dad—this is how we talk. We talk in food."

"You both are cracked," I mutter.

"Eat," my dad says. "We will do the talking thing after."

So I eat. It tastes good—or at least, as good as something I'm not hungry for can taste. I manage to choke down two crepes, some bacon, and about four sips of fresh-squeezed juice. Then I push my plate away and say, "Now we talk."

My father goes first.

"Stella, your behavior last night—it was inexcusable."

"I know," I groan. "I'm sorry, Dad. Really, I—"

"Let me finish," he says. "Your behavior *was* inexcusable. But what you said about me lying, leaving—these things are true. I should have told you about Masha sooner. And I should have, long ago, talked to you about why I left."

"*We* should've talked to you," Mom corrects him, placing her hand over Dad's. "The thing is, Stel, we both tried really hard to make our breakup as painless for you as possible. But I guess in doing so, we never fully broke up."

"This is why I am here this morning," Dad says. "Your mother and I—we are getting the divorce."

"You've supposedly been getting 'the divorce' for the past six years," I remind him.

"What your father means," Mom says, "is that it's officially in the works, Stella. It takes a while to finalize these things. But it *is* happening. And it should've happened a lot sooner. I'm sorry that it didn't. I'm sorry that we didn't let you get closure on our breakup."

The word "breakup" hits me hard. My parents are divorcing. They've broken up. They're seeing other people.

They've fallen completely out of love.

Mom starts crying almost as soon as I do. She comes to me and wraps her arms around me and tells me how much she loves me, how much they both love me.

Dad says, "We love each other, too. Your mother and

me. We just learned that we cannot be in love. We do not work that way. Do you understand?"

I nod, sniffing back some snot. "I think so."

Now it's Dad's turn to hug me. "I love you, Stella-belle. You must know that you are the most important thing to me. This is not going to change."

"We know this will take time," Mom says. "But you must—"

"I will," I interject. "I will be okay. Not today, but eventually."

I want to get away from them, be by myself for a while so I can process everything that's happened in the past twenty-four hours. But when I say, "I think I'm going to go to my room now," my mother tells me to wait a minute.

"You're not off the hook," she says. "You stole alcohol. You got drunk at the Kitchen, which put my business at risk. You embarrassed us in front of your friends—"

"And yours," I interject sourly.

"Watch your mouth," Dad says.

"I know that you know what you did was very, very wrong. But there are additional consequences here."

My punishment is relatively light considering the crime: in addition to apologizing to Vince, Masha, and Enrique, I will be spending all my free time for the next two weeks at the Kitchen. Basically, doing all the menial tasks I was responsible for before I started my internship.

"There's something else," Mom says. "We'd like you to consider going to some family counseling sessions with us. You know, to work through our feelings."

Dad pulls a face; I can tell this is Mom's idea, not his.

"You on board with this, Dad?"

He nods. "I want what is best for you."

"Okay, then. I'll do it. *Now* can I go to my room?"

"Sure," Mom says. "*After* you've done the dishes, of course."

Good to know that some things never change.

EPILOGUE

MENU FOR THURSDAY, AUGUST 13
Chef André Madison of Mélange
"Remembering Julia Child"
*Oysters broiled in garlic butter; classic Niçoise salad and French
bread; sole Meunière served with blanched and buttered green
beans and potatoes Anna; chocolate mousse*

It was love at first sight.

Mom and I were at a stoplight last Saturday, heading back to the apartment after our fifth and final family counseling session with Dad, when I saw it: a 1994 teal blue Toyota Corolla glinting in the sunlight. The price was painted in red against a yellow starburst that took up most of the windshield. It read: "$1,998.00—cash only."

"Stop the car!" I squealed. "I mean, turn into that lot! Please!"

Mom sighed but did as I asked. "Which one are you looking at?"

"That one." I pointed out the Toyota. "They're on your list of acceptable makes, right?"

Ninety minutes and one test drive later I walked out

of Newark Toyotaworld the proud owner of a genuine, certified, preowned, Consumer Reports–rated, Mom-approved car—bought with money I earned at the *Daily Journal*, of course.

Because of a snafu with the stereo system's installation, I wasn't able to take possession until today. I used that time to come up with a name for my very first car, and after much careful consideration decided on Tess, which is the name of the character Mrs. Antonio Banderas played in *Working Girl*. It seemed like a fitting choice.

Since the paperwork was processed when I purchased Tess last week, Mom agrees to let Kat and Olivia drive me to the dealership to pick her up.

"This is a monumental occasion," Kat says as we pull into the lot.

"I know," Livvy says. "Our girl's all grown up!"

"With your first car comes great responsibility," Kat adds gravely. "Are you sure you can handle it?"

"You're joking, right?" I say. "No longer will I have to scrounge rides off the two of you. I thought you'd be thrilled!"

"Oh, we're thrilled, all right," Livvy says. "You're our chauffeur now."

"I call shotgun!" Kat chimes in.

I add Tess's two keys to the new pink-rhinestone-encrusted "S" key ring my mother gave me this morning as a car-warming present.

"Thanks for the ride," I tell Kat. "Hopefully I won't need to say that again for a while."

"Amen, sister," Liv quips.

The girls wait while I adjust the seat and mirrors, strap on my seat belt, and start her up. Tess purrs happily as I pull out of the lot and onto Ogletown Road. I turn the radio on and scan the stations until I land on XPN. Feist's "I Feel It All" pours out from the speakers and floods my veins. I do know more than I did before, I think. And no one can break my heart better than I can.

Tess isn't the only reason that today is monumental. My internship ended this morning, after I turned my final "What's Cooking" column in to Mike Hardwick. Earlier this month he asked if I'd stay on as a freelancer for the *Snap!* staff, but I turned him down.

"I'm flattered," I told him. "But it's my senior year. Between school and helping out at the Kitchen and applying to colleges . . ."

"I understand," he said. "I'm disappointed, but I get it. Well, maybe you'll consider coming back next summer. I hear you have an interest in writing about music?"

This last column was the hardest for me to write. It's a personal essay titled "The F-Word"—thirty column inches about how hard it was growing up the junk-food-loving daughter of two famous foodies, and how before this summer I never realized that I was actually one of them. But I couldn't tell that story without including Jeremy, and before I knew it, this is what I'd written:

The great playwright George Bernard Shaw once wrote, "There is no love sincerer than the love of food." But I disagree. Because in my family, there's no love sincerer than the kind expressed through food. Not even two months ago, my parents, who had been separated since I was twelve years old, sat me down to tell me they were finalizing the divorce. My father catered the event with homemade crepes, the ones he learned to make from his mother, who learned from her mother.

I'd eaten these crepes dozens of times growing up, but I never truly tasted them until three weeks ago—the day my parents signed their divorce papers. That's when I asked my father if he would teach me how to make them myself.

If you've never made crepes before, you should try it: they're a lot easier than they look. All you need are eggs, flour, milk, butter, and salt—things most people already have in their kitchen.

But there is one ingredient not listed on most recipes, and that is patience, an indispensable ingredient in <u>any</u> recipe, as a good friend of mine recently taught me. Preparing the perfect crepe requires you to heat a skillet slowly, over low to medium heat. You can only use a scant amount of batter—no more than a quarter cup—which then gets swirled around the hot pan. You can only flip them once, but you can't flip them before they're ready (you'll know because they start to look like lace) or else they'll fall apart.

If you think about it, falling in love is a lot like making crepes. The recipe is fairly simple, but if you try to rush the process, you'll only end up with a soggy mess.

> Then again, if you take your time, and if you
> learn from the mistakes you will undoubtedly
> make on those first few batches, odds are you'll
> end up with something a lot more satisfying.

I let my parents read the piece before submitting it to Mike, to make sure they were okay with me exposing so much of their personal lives publicly. Both gave their blessing. It was sort of healing, actually, to put it all down on paper. Even our family therapist approved.

The third thing that makes today monumental is tonight's dinner at the Kitchen. It's an open event, but most of the seats have been filled by invitation. *My* invitation. Dad's cooking, and he told me to bring my friends so we can celebrate my new car in style. Kat, Livvy, and Omar are meeting me there. I even invited Max, but he declined politely. Kat says he's still licking his wounds, but Liv said she saw him last week sharing a gelato at Rita's with Allison, this supercute cheerleader one grade below us.

That's not all. Masha's taking the train in from New York, and I asked Vince to bring August, whom I haven't met yet, as Mom told me she'd wait until I was ready.

I suppose I'm as ready as I'll ever be.

Jeremy's is the first face I see when I step into the Kitchen. He flashes me a warm, friendly smile instead of a flirty one, but I'm okay with that. We've been working on the friendship thing since the night of our one and only kiss, and it's nice. I haven't had many guy friends who were just that: *friends*.

"So what's for dinner?" I say. "I'm *starving*."

ACKNOWLEDGMENTS

This book wouldn't exist if not for the inspiration of three people: Angela Martinez and Cindy Weiner, who own and operate the very real Celebrity Kitchens in Wilmington, Delaware, and Chef Phil Pyle of the Fair Hill Inn, whom I met during one of the many dinners I've had at Celebrity Kitchens, and whose excellent storytelling skills—not to mention culinary prowess—made me say, "Someday I'm going to put that man in a novel."

But while I shamelessly stole the setting of this book from Celebrity Kitchens, and gave Stella's dad Chef Phil's philosophy of cooking, this is primarily a work of fiction, and neither Amy nor André Madison (nor anyone else in this book) is meant to represent a real-life person.

Actually, I need to amend my earlier statement, as this book also would not exist without my editor, Jodi Keller. When I told her, "I want to write a book about a girl named Stella. I think her dad might be a chef," she said, "Go with it." Jodi, thank you for trusting me, and for helping me make this book the best it could be. I would also like to thank Beverly Horowitz, who encouraged this exploration of foodie culture long before *Top Chef* became a hit show on cable TV.

As always, I owe so much to my agent, George

Nicholson, who has faith in me even when I don't have it in myself. Also to Laurie Stolarz and the members of the WIPs—Carolee, Chris, Cindy, Gale, Jane, Jo, and Shannon—all of whom read many drafts of this project and offered valuable support, encouragement, and feedback every step of the way.

Much gratitude goes out to my parents, true foodies in every sense of the word—especially my momma, who's not only responsible for introducing me to Celebrity Kitchens and Chef Phil, but who also taught me how to scramble eggs.

Finally, there's Joe, my sous-chef for life—writing about love became a million times easier once I met you. You're my favorite everything, and I adore you with all my heart.

ABOUT THE AUTHOR

Lara Zeises is the author of *Bringing Up the Bones*, a Delacorte Press Prize Honor Book; *Contents Under Pressure*, a Delaware Blue Hen Book Award winner and an IRA-CBC Young Adults' Choice; and *Anyone but You*. She is the recipient of an Emerging Artist Fellowship in Literature—Fiction from the Delaware Division of the Arts, and earned her MFA in creative writing from Emerson College.

Lara has also published two novels under the pseudonym Lola Douglas: *True Confessions of a Hollywood Starlet*, which was adapted into a Lifetime movie starring multiplatinum recording artist Joanna "JoJo" Levesque and Golden Globe Award–winning actress Valerie Bertinelli, and its sequel, *More Confessions of a Hollywood Starlet*.

In addition to writing, Lara enjoys playing Iron Chef in her own kitchen, especially when the secret ingredient is bacon. She worships at the altar of Alton Brown but credits her mother with turning her into an avid home cook and bona fide foodie.

Lara lives in Delaware, where she grew up, but you can visit her online at www.zeisgeist.com.